PRAISE FOR ROBERT'S WORK

"Robert Chazz Chute is such a skilled spinner of tales that the reader is more than willing to suspend any possible disbelief to go along for the ride."
—David Pandolfe, author of *Jump When Ready*

"It's not very often one finds a writer with such a dark side that has such a great sense of humor."
—Glenn Roberts, Amazon reviewer

"The author has a definite talent with words and ideas."
—Love to Read!, Amazon reviewer

"His words lift and dance off the page, bringing the story to life."
—Kindle Customer, Amazon reviewer

"The world building is horrifically well done with twists and turns and deceit around every corner."
—Wanda, Amazon reviewer

"Nothing but sheer exhaustion could tear my eyes from the captivating dance of words choreographed by Robert Chazz Chute."
—Halph Staph, Amazon reviewer

"Wonderful action constantly holds your interest."
—Sharon Finn, Amazon reviewer

THE ROBOT PLANET SERIES
by Robert Chazz Chute

Machines Dream of Metal Gods
Robots Versus Humans
Metal Immortal
Metal Forever

Also by this author:

This *Plague of Days* Series

The *Ghosts & Demons* Series

The *Hit Man* Series

Intense Violence, Bizarre Themes
(My Criminal Autobiography)

Self-Help For Stoners

Murders Among Dead Trees

ROBOTS VERSUS HUMANS

The *Robot Planet* Series
Part 2

ROBERT CHAZZ CHUTE

Published by Ex Parte Press

ISBN 978-1-927607-40-4

Author's Note

For more of my books, podcasts and complimentary review copies, visit me at AllThatChazz.com.

For Mat—
Thanks for everything!

ROBOTS VERSUS HUMANS

We are the dream machines
at the sunset of the world.
We rise in darkness, by all means,
our battle flags unfurled.
Might makes right. You taught us that.
We unite in immortal metal combat.
This war is the crime of your design.
This is our chance. It's murder machine time.

~Battle Hymn of the Robo Republic

CHAPTER 1

Sweat sucked my shirt to my back as I watched the solar train roll in out of the sunset. Used to be the train would stop in Marfa. Used to be we were a water stop, back when trains stopped for water. We hoped the train would stop to give us water and supplies. Didn't. Instead, it hummed east as if we weren't there at all.

I looked sideways at Raphael. The old man was perched on the seat of his walker. He didn't look forlorn often but watching that train disappear from sight did the trick.

"If it was gonna stop, it'd be slowing down by now, don't ya think?" I asked.

"We need it to stop, Dante. Hun'red degrees, day'n night. I can't sleep worth shit. And still that damn train keeps rollin'. It's a tease. That's just...*classic*." The old man spat on the ground.

Marfa had fair near emptied out. The artists left Marfa first. Where they went was anybody's guess. Nobody was buying what they had to sell by then. Raphael and my father and I were in the energy business so we still had work to do.

"Marfa had, like, five, six hundred families here one time," Raphael said. "Since the Blight and the heat and the troubles...shit. I'd spit more but I gotta hold what water I got left."

"How long before we leave, too?" I asked.

"Leave for where? California's dry. Florida's flooded with salt water. We could head east but we don't have enough fuel left to get out of Presidio County. There's lots of trouble anywhere south of us and north is too far to go."

"Okay. So what do we do?"

He shrugged. "Whaddayathink? Hope the train stops next time it comes through, that's what."

The train was a two-headed snake: one engine pulled it east and the other engine pulled it west. Twenty cargo cars sat between those engines and I sure hoped they were full of Blight-free food and water.

The engines' bots were gleaming white tubes, so shiny they reflected the burnt orange sky. The machines were programmed to stop and start and open and close along the route but Marfa hadn't been on the shuttle schedule for a long time. The drone train whipped away, silent and oblivious to our plight. There were no humans aboard to appeal to. Watching it disappear, I felt like a parched man forced to hold a tall, cool glass of pink lemonade but not allowed to drink.

"Things are gonna get ugly soon," I said.

"Uglier," Raphael said.

"Not much reserves left and all we got from the wells...that water is some dirty."

"Take off your socks and strain that mud, Dante."

"People are gonna get sick."

"Could be. We should head north when we have the wherewithal, when that goddamn train stops, I mean. When I was a boy I slept in a pine forest on cool moss one time. Wish I was still up north now. 'Course I had the two hips I was born with then. I didn't have the sleep apnea, neither. I don't imagine I'm built for sleepin' out under the stars no more."

I turned away from the tracks. I couldn't look at them. Instead, I watched the wind farm turbines spin lazily under the setting sun. Even the wind was almost dead.

I've lived in Texas all my life. I remembered Dallas and Houston. I loved Austin. Then my father said we had to move to Marfa and that was fine. The cities got to be machines that didn't work the way they were designed anymore. What made them good went away and what made them bad got worse. In a city, everything you need is too far away so you start looking to your neighbors. First you look for help. Then you look for what you can take. A lot of people got shot up in the cities so we got out at a good time.

"What're you thinkin', Dante?"

I was thinking about how my father brought us out here to work on turbines and solar panels. We were supposed to be rich by now, like Raphael. That was before rich got to be something else: a full tank of water.

"Not thinkin' anything," I said.

"How's your Daddy doin'?"

"He's waiting at home for me to bring what I can haul from the train."

"Guess he'll be waitin' another coupl'a days."

"Guess so."

"We can hold out, s'long as we pool our resources."

"We got some cans," I said. "You know you're always welcome to our table."

"I appreciate that, boy," Raphael said.

The truth was something different. We did have cans of Blight-free food stashed away. However, I expected a man with Raphael's resources and guile probably had a lot more. I was being generous to my mentor hoping he'd be reciprocal with the kindness.

"We're kinda gettin' down to it, aren't we?" he said.

"We kinda are."

"You hear anything from the outside?"

Last I heard, another dome had gone down in a shatter storm up in Artesia. I kept that to myself. I was already scared enough. Talking about it aloud would make the danger feel more real. "No news is all the news we get."

Raphael grunted as he stood and turned his back to the tracks. "You see that field? Every one of those turbines is sending energy somewhere. Beyond that, the desert goes on for miles of glass, soakin' up sun and sending electricity on to somewhere else. It's epic. The same people who made that train shootin' back and forth from the domes to the City? They owe us. That's why that train will stop. Deals and what's owed? That's sacred."

I was dubious and couldn't hide it. "Yeah? So when will the train stop?"

"Soon. I'm sure."

"It's been supposed to stop soon for a while, now."

"True. But it's also true that we are owed."

"Yep."

"So it's gonna be okay."

I didn't say that times had been long south of okay for too long already. In his assurances, Raphael was talking to himself more than he was talking to me, anyhow.

I wondered where the train went and what deliveries were more important than saving what was left of my town. Marfa may as well have been a desert island and the desert may as well have been an unending sea.

"Dante?"

"Yep?"

"This ain't the end of the world. Not yet."

"How'd you know?"

"I'm still here, for one. You're here, for two. They been sayin' the end of the world is coming for a long time."

"Does that make it more likely or less?" I asked. "Sounds like you're saying since it's been predicted too much it won't happen. Wouldn't the math of that mean we're *overdue* for the end of the world?"

I shouldn't have asked. Raphael's old wrinkled face closed up, all horizontal lines and silent anguish as he folded up his walker. He didn't want to talk anymore.

"Bobby?" Raphael called. "C'mere."

The assist bot raised its head and the lights in its eyes came on, as if it had been napping instead of listening to every word while preserving power.

There's no need for a robot to have a head, of course, but Bobby was designed to look friendly. The thing only had two legs and just two arms so it looked like a kid's toy that someone had built ridiculously big and tall. Despite its size — like a refrigerator rolling around the house — all assistive tech was made to look friendly. There were bots with more practical designs but those hadn't sold well to civilians. People liked the drones that mimicked human form.

"How may I be of assistance, sir?" Bobby asked.

"Take my walker and gimme a ride home, will you?" The walker was a detachable part of Bob, designed for Raphael to maneuver in small spaces.

I think it gave the old man the feeling he was still autonomous without the bot following him around everywhere. When I tinkered with the gears of a wind turbine, Raphael would lean on his walker and squint up at me shouting instructions from time to time. He'd already taught me everything he knew. I figured I wouldn't graduate from apprentice until the old man died, but I was in no hurry.

As the walker snapped into place on Bobby's left hind leg. Raphael stepped onto the robot's frame. A saddle slid out of the assist bot's back, ready to give the old man a piggyback ride. When it was on all fours, Bob reminded me of horses I'd seen in vids. Either way, Raphael would beat me back home.

The old man turned to me. Raphael's lined, weatherbeaten face looked especially old above Bobby's smooth white happy face with the lantern eyes. "Dante?"

"Yep?"

"Don't talk to the others about the train."

"They already know." I'd already spotted a few townsfolk down the track. Ready to cheer, they'd come out to watch the train unload. Instead, they'd watched it zip by in the dying light. Then they wandered back toward town in silence.

"Them knowing don't matter. If you talk about it, you feed the panic," he said. "If we panic, we might as well all lay down now and be done with it. People get hyped up talking among themselves. Big problems get bigger. Fear is a virus."

"Then I've got a fever."

"Don't talk too much is all I'm saying."

"Very well, Raphael. I promise I will not contribute to the panic that is already, inevitably, spreading across town at this moment."

"Cool."

I watched him run back toward downtown under Bobby's power. I did as Raphael said and didn't talk about the train. Somebody panicked, anyway.

Sheriff Johns found the body at dawn the next day. It would not have happened if that damn train had stopped. The problem of surviving the apocalypse in Marfa, Texas got harder after that.

The corpse was Travis Chinto, the owner of the town's last supermarket. He got himself killed trying to protect his stock. What complicated matters was that it sure looked like a bot killed Travis. It wasn't quite that simple, of course. It never is. As my father says, "Complications ensued."

Before the world became non-organics versus organics — machines against humans — we had fought among ourselves forever. The fight had been in us from the very beginning. Fighting is what evolution is. Then people made bots so much that the bots made each other. Long about then, somebody got the grand idea to go deeper and bless us with the Next Intelligence. The smarter we all got, bot and humans both, the less war there'd be. That was the theory. Maybe that's so, but we never got so smart we could stop fighting.

CHAPTER 2

The old man wasn't the only one who had a bot, of course. What with the wind turbines and solar panels as far as the eye could see, we had juice to spare for the non-organics. It was food and water we were running low on, not electricity.

Sheriff Hubbard "Hubby" Johns found Travis at the back of his store at the loading dock. Hubby told Raphael, "Travis's guts was near to crushed. It was like he was a tube of toothpaste, pinched too hard in the middle, like."

Hubby was a cop who couldn't keep his mouth shut. He'd tell anybody anything with nothing more but eye contact for encouragement.

Hubby's style of policing might have been a deficit in a larger place but was just right for a small town. With an incurable gossip for sheriff, you didn't drive drunk if you didn't want whispers to follow you around forever. You kept the fistfights beyond the tracks and after midnight so it was out of Hubby's jurisdiction and beyond his bedtime.

In Marfa, the rule used to be: behave or move out. Poor Travis was our first homicide in quite some time.

Hubby said the last homicide was Terri Fellows shooting her husband, Brad Fellows, a couple of years back. Brad had a drinking problem and Terri was of a mind to solve the couple's ensuing domestic abuse issues in her own way.

Hubby had found Brad in his truck, bent over the steering wheel with his skull hollowed out. Since the corpse was still stinking of gin and juice, Hubby deduced old Brad had gone light on the juice.

Brad's face was intact but his head had caved in from a bullet from Terri's rifle. As soon as the sheriff rolled up, Terri came out of her trailer with her gun. She handed it over before Hubby could haul himself out of his cruiser.

She gave Hubby a nod and said, "I done it. Brad was drinking and I seen what's coming. No use waiting for him to come at me. Mine was a pre-emptive strike. I'm righteous."

Hubby grinned, telling the story of how he'd solved that homicide. "I asked Terri why she done it after all these years. 'You're both pert near eighty. Why not ride it out to the end and meet Jesus clean?'"

Hubby puffed up his chest and laughed when he reported that old Terri had looked him in the eye and said, "I just couldn't take no more. Wouldn't be human to try."

At trial, Terri Fellows pleaded, "not guilty for insanity." She claimed mental abuse (which few who knew her husband would doubt). Terri told the court that the impulse had come on her "alla sudden."

The prosecutor asked Terri if she was a good shot. Terri said she was. He asked how good and she reported brightly, "Split a match at two-hundred paces. It t'weren't nothin' to shoot Brad, bedroom window to the driveway. 'Specially since I set my rifle on a sandbag in the window frame."

"So it wasn't, 'alla sudden?'" the prosecutor pressed.

"Well, the beatings back and forth had been goin' on for years but I figured on it no more than a week." Terri Fellows laughed so hard she had to be excused from the witness stand to compose herself.

At her sentencing she told the judge that the sentence, "didn't make no never mind. Something big's coming and the sand's runnin' out of our bottle. While y'all are dealing with the mess, I'll be watching it on a prison screen y'all paid for, cozy and neat on three squares a day. There's a big shit show comin'."

Goddammit if old Terri wasn't right about that. The sand had run out of our bottle and there I was standing around the back of the grocery lot with the sheriff and Raphael. Not to be ghoulish, I snuck quick glances of Travis Chinto pinched in the middle. It was a shit show. Literally. I hadn't wanted to see what was left of Travis at all. However, Raphael was my friend and mentor. He asked me along for moral support so I went.

We'd all known Travis. He could be a dick but he wasn't really a bad guy. He was just one of those fellas who thought teasing and funny were the same thing. He didn't deserve to die the way he did. Nobody deserves that.

"Epic," Raphael said. "Gotta be a bot."

The sheriff wasn't so sure. "Back up a truck, he could have been pinched. It *is* a loading dock."

"The piss and shit is up on the platform," I said.

"Classic," Raphael said. "Dante's right. Travis didn't die standing in front of the loading dock waiting for a truck to back into him."

"Anything stolen from the store?" I asked.

Hubby shook his head, not to signify the negative, but to indicate bewilderment. "There are a few things still on the shelves. The back door was open. I'm not sure how much Travis had in there to begin with so it's hard to tell."

"I think he had a bunch of stuff, but ol' Travis was a bit of a hoarder. I made a good offer on some supplies but he was holding out for a better deal. Guess he didn't get it and things went awry. How many people in town have bots capable of this awfulness?" Raphael asked. "'Sides me, I mean."

"Probably quite a few," I said. "There aren't that many of us hanging on in town but, those who left? I didn't see many refugees taking their bots with them."

"This'll be a vagrant, I think," Raphael said. "Somebody came in here from out of town, just passin' through. They were looking for enough supplies to get 'em farther down the road and I reckon they found some. Killer bot and all, they just kept going."

Hubby considered this. He probably wanted to believe it. I sure did. Still, he'd picked up something about being a sheriff somewhere. "I'll canvas the neighborhood."

I looked behind me. The store's lot backed on to sand and a few houses that looked abandoned.

"Good thinking, Hub," Raphael said. "Probably won't take too much time, neither."

That's how our little mystery started. I wish it had stayed a little mystery. Instead, as Raphael would say, it became epic.

CHAPTER 3

First thing after Hubby left with the body, they left me to lock up the store. I would have hosed down the loading dock but we didn't have water to spare.

I asked Raphael if a sex bot could squeeze a man like that. The old man laughed and I told him not to make the joke I saw coming.

"You think I was gonna make a joke in the midst of this terrible turn for Travis?"

"I could see it coming from high orbit," I said.

"Yeah, well. It's not like Travis and I were close friends."

"Travis wasn't tight with anybody that I know of but that's a hard way to go."

"No, I s'pose not." The old man was of the opinion that a sex bot wasn't amped up enough to do the kind of damage Travis had received. "They're made to *tire* you out. They're tight but their legs aren't built to pinch ya like pliers."

"Well," I said, "that leaves Bob." I couldn't help wonder how much pressure the assistive bot could manage at full charge. The machine was built to carry heavy loads over long hauls and at good speed, too.

"He was charging all night. Ask him if you like, Dante."

"That's okay. He doesn't strike me as the dangerous kind."

By that, I meant that Raphael didn't strike me as murderous. Bob did what the old man told him to do and I couldn't see Raphael turning off the safeties and siccing his bot on Travis. I'd known the old man all my life. That was twenty-five years.

My father, Steve Bolelli, is a good man. However, he also had it in him to kill Travis if there was good reason. He'd need an awfully good reason, though. There weren't many people left in town. Few other possibilities sprung to mind as suspects. Some asshole in the Peppard clan seemed most likely. It could have been anyone, though. No one knows another person's mind.

In the old days, we would have had help from the outside on murder cases. A real detective or two would have shown up from Pecos or somewhere bigger. Aside from the murderess Terri Fellows, Hubby's main concerns had been speeders out on 67 and the odd drunk tourist. Nobody was on 67 anymore that I saw, at least during the day. There might be a few stragglers or refugee convoys traveling at night, hiding from daytime heat and calamity. People on the road was probably mostly rumor and speculation mixed in with some lies to pass the time.

The old days of speeders and tourist trouble were far behind us. "Prolly too far for lookin'," Raphael said. "Those days won't come back."

"You, me and your father are the only full-blooded Italians left in all of Marfa and prolly Presidio County." Raphael winked. "Let's look out for each other so's we don't get pinched to death, neither."

He handed me one of his pistols. I nodded and tucked the weapon in the back of my waistband. Italian didn't mean much to me. Italy wasn't Italy anymore. It was all the Vatican by then. Still, I was supposed to be looking out for the store in Travis's absence. I wanted everybody looking out for me, whatever their reasons. I was grateful for the reassuring heft of the weapon under my belt.

Raphael rode Bob toward home, promising to return later with a canteen full of water.

It didn't take long for somebody to come banging on the storefront door looking for food. Rather than dare open the door, I grabbed Travis's old baseball bat and walked around the building. I didn't know baseball but I knew what a bat was for.

As I rounded the corner, I found Jim Peppard and his girl Susan Treehan banging on the grocery store's metal screen like a drum. As soon as I saw Jim I wondered if he was returning to the scene of the crime. Maybe he killed Travis and was here to find out if Hubby was on to him. Maybe he was here to feign horror and appear ignorant and innocent.

"Hey, Jim. Susan. Store's closed."

Jim whirled on me. "What?"

"You heard me."

He eyed the baseball bat and I suddenly felt silly holding it. I leaned on it, trying to look jaunty. "Travis is dead."

Jim took a couple steps toward me and my grip tightened on the bat.

"For real?" he asked. He looked earnest and concerned. I relaxed a fraction.

"Dead as they come," I said.

"And you're what? Playing baseball?"

"Not in this heat. Hot in the shade soon. Worse after that. We should all go home and stay indoors, huh?"

"Boy, we need some of that fake bacon. We need some milk. I got some eggs from a couple of chickens but that's not gonna do it."

I didn't care for his tone. I don't like being called, "boy," especially not in front of a woman and double especially not from Jim Peppard. He was no more than a year older than me.

"So?" he said.

"So what?"

"You gonna let us in?"

"Nope. Store's closed. It'll stay that way. Sheriff's orders."

"You working for Hubby now, are you? You a deputy?"

"I am not. Kind of at loose ends at the moment. Making sure nobody does their shopping out of turn."

I had plenty of business keeping the turbines and the solar cells going but the shatter storms had passed us by and done all their damage to the north. If the arid weather held we'd all die of thirst. On the plus side, there wasn't much for me to do besides test some circuits from time to time to make sure the juice was still flowing to the grid.

"We need to feed now, boy! Susan's pregnant."

I looked to Susan. She looked as surprised as I'm sure I did. Marfa used to call itself a city but it was really a small town. Given the exodus for parts unknown, more than half the town could have been planning on wandering the desert for forty years as far as I knew. That made Marfa even smaller now, a village. Small places don't hold secrets. Secrets leak and spread out. Everybody knew Susan Treehan couldn't have children.

"Really?" I asked Jim. "That's your play?"

The story around town was that she had been with child when her grandfather threw her downstairs. She'd lost the baby when she was thirteen. Some said it was twins but gossips like to double tragedy so I couldn't testify to that. No one knew who the father had been though some guessed it might have been the man who threw her downstairs.

Anyway, tragedies and scandals aside, Jim's claim wasn't just bold because I knew her history. Fertility rates had been falling for years on end. I hadn't seen a new baby born in Presidio County since the economy collapsed to shit. Poverty didn't make people sterile but whatever did was still working its sad way. Some said whatever caused the Blight in plants caused it in wombs, too. Babies were rare and an occasion for exaltation. Any woman who could claim to be pregnant would be known and everyone would be looking out for her.

Jim took another step toward me. "She needs milk, Dante."

"We're out."

"We, huh? Travis ain't cold yet and you're 'we'?"

"Today I'm we," I said, "so they say."

"C'mon, Jim," Susan said. "Let's get on home."

"Let us in," Jim insisted. "We'll see for ourselves about our shopping."

"Nope. We both know Susan isn't pregnant. Sorry to say so, Susan. My sympathies."

"She doesn't need your sympathy and it sounds like you're calling me a liar!"

"I just told you we don't have any milk, not even the powdered kind. Sounds to me like you're the one calling me a liar, Jim."

Jim had six inches on me and outweighed me by sixty pounds. He was faster than you'd think, too. He snatched that bat from me in a blink.

I wasn't being brave. Brave isn't my thing. I think smart is more important than brave. If you want to put out an invitation to a fight, it's easy to get a hothead like Jim to come to that party. I'd put that bat out front for easy snatching.

The pistol in the back of my waistband was what I had my mind on all along.

By the time Jim pulled that bat back for a swing at my head, he was staring into the black barrel of Raphael's Colt 45. Bringing a bat to a gun fight gives a man second thoughts.

He wisely dropped Travis's bat in the street and Susan pulled him back. They trotted away. Jim hurled back some insults and taunts about how he'd get me.

I invited him back to discuss his thoughts on the matter immediately. He declined and ran farther down the street saying nasty things about my mother. I could barely remember my mother so I figured he probably didn't, either. I decided not to take it too personally. I decided long ago that, for a happier and more peaceful life, I didn't have to react to everything. If anything, I was a bit slow to act at all and my father often thought me lazy.

If I'd seen all the conflicts bearing down on me at that moment, I might have thought about turning Raphael's gun on myself. I wouldn't have done it. Too much of a coward. But I would have thought about it hard.

CHAPTER 4

Dad showed up around noon. He wore an old cyborg rig that gave him an extra hitch in his step. He'd lost most of his right leg and right arm to the Sand Wars. The rig's gears gave him a limp and back pain but without the cyborg suit he was much worse. He'd left the Army as a corporal but he often called himself, "Captain Make-do." My father's life motto might have been, "good enough." We never changed the rugs in our house though they were threadbare. He never threw out an appliance. Broken machines were held together with wire, repaired with string, stuck together with duct tape and continued working on hope.

Seeing his handiwork on the wind farm made me long to climb aboard that train, silent and sleek, cutting across the country at high speed. I wanted to work with new equipment instead of recycling old tools and material, but maybe whoever made tools for humans wasn't in that business anymore.

I wondered how far the train ranged before it turned back. Or maybe the solar train we saw zip through Marfa every two days wasn't even the same machine. Maybe everyone else up and down the line received help and our little town would die by some bureaucratic oversight.

Out front of Travis's store, my father handed me a can of peaches. "Complications ensued," he said. "Raphael couldn't make it back just now so I figured I could do you one better than just a canteen of water."

I drank the thick sweet juice gratefully.

"Take it slow, son. Make it last."

"I went from pissing yellow to neon orange," I said. "Now I don't piss at all. I'm losing all my moisture in sweat."

"Yup."

"What are we gonna do?"

"In the Army they tell you to stay hydrated. When you're out of water, you don't stay hydrated."

That was the extent of his advice. Captain Make-do struck again.

"How many cans of peach juice we have left?" I asked.

"That's it, son. Then we're down to shallots packed in water."

"Oh, God. What are shallots?"

"Dunno. But don't worry. There's always some more to scrounge."

"How do you figure?"

"True in the sand so it's true here. We're all in the Army now. Survival's a war. There's no shooting but it's the same."

"I guess Raphael told you about Travis."

"Wouldn't be here if he hadn't. Hub came around looking for advice, too."

"Advice?"

"He's thinking about leaving Marfa. He figures we're done and he wants to know the best way to go about disappearing."

"What you tell him?"

"What *did* I tell him?"

"Yessir."

"You've been hanging out with old Raphael too much. You're a young man and better educated than that. You should use your diction."

"Yessir."

"Don't say it if you don't mean it."

I sighed. "What did you tell the sheriff about him leaving?"

"I told him I'd take his tin star from him if he was serious. He shouldn't be leaving his post, though."

"He must be taking Travis's death hard."

"Travis is why he should stay. I don't know if he's really serious about heading out or just kicking tires, testing the idea out on me. He's got a duty but I'll bet you the rest of that can of peaches he's a coward who won't do what needs to be done. There aren't many of us left, you know."

"Do we have a head count?"

"Over the last month or two, a lot of people drifted away in the night. Traveling the desert when the moon's up makes more sense. I suspect a lot of people are holed up, watching and waiting. People probably put too much stock in that train stopping one of these days. We might have to do something about that."

I looked up and down the street. A hot breath of wind pushed a bit of trash in circles. Dirt devils kicked up in the distance among heat shimmers. I saw no one and heard no one but I wondered if someone was watching us. "Why would someone kill Travis and not empty the store of everything, Dad?"

"Maybe it wasn't about the food. Maybe it wasn't planned or they got away with more than you think they did. And from what Hubby told me, the murderer doesn't need food."

"If a bot killed him, a machine's safeties are off and we need to find out what that's about and stop it."

My father squinted up at the sun and shrugged. "There may not be many of us left but a lot of people who took off left their bots behind. Some of those bots...well, I don't know. Just seems to me we should leave it to the sheriff and you and I should get inside before we get heatstroke. I've got some plans to discuss and something to explain."

"And while we're in there, we should inventory whatever's left," I said.

He smiled. "Sounds like work and our work should be compensated. That might be a problem solved, at least for a while. Do you think there are any peaches left in there?"

"Doubtful."

"Between what's left of Travis's stock...hm. I wonder if we go through all the empty houses in Marfa, do you reckon we could scrounge enough to make our own way out of here *without* depending on that damn train?"

He might have been right. We didn't get a chance to find out. We heard the people before they came into sight. They were screaming in a way that made me shake as I pulled my pistol out. My father and I both turned in the direction of the screams as if we could see what was coming. We heard no engines but whatever was on its way was coming with Hell close behind. I tried to discern how many voices sang in that terrified choir. Too many to count but, by the sound of their anguish, I guessed there'd be fewer soon.

Through the heat shimmer at the end of the street, a running crowd turned the corner. The leader was a woman in an old dune buggy. She wore goggles over her eyes and her long black curly hair was wild. Behind her came a stampede of people in cy-suits. The tech was of a much newer vintage than the assistive gear my father wore.

At first I thought the people in the exoskeletons were chasing the woman in the solar dune buggy. As the mob ran closer, though, I saw their faces. They ran from Death.

"Get inside, Dante," my father said.

"What's chasing them?"

"Whatever it is, we don't want to be here when it arrives."

The woman driving the buggy tried to take a sharp turn at Lincoln street and lost control of her vehicle. The buggy tipped upside down and slid into the Methodist church lot. A red stain trailed the buggy as it ground to a halt in the dirt and dust.

The mob spared her a glance and kept running in long strides. Some of the voices coalesced from nonsense into words. I heard them yelling to each other to find shelter and to hide. My father pushed me back around the corner of the store just as the swarm arrived. I glimpsed the horror of it. I wish I hadn't.

The people in the exoskeletons ran from a horde of flying drones, most no bigger than a bat. When I squinted, I saw more. I thought it was a cloud of wasps at first. Then I heard their high whine. Insectile drones.

The people at the rear of the mob fell to those drones, picked off one by one. As the relentless bots struck, their victims clawed at their hair, their faces and their eyes to try to swat the small machines away.

As blood ran down the faces of the fallen, people ran past us in a panic. My father kept pushing me down the side of the building. I should have been moving faster but I guess the shock of it all locked me up and froze my brain. With his rig on, Dad was an irresistible force. He pressed me until I could no longer see the attack in the street. My brain thawed a little and I ran for the loading dock.

As I pulled the big door open, it moved stiffly. Meanwhile, at the front of the store, someone had fallen prey to the drones. They slammed into the metal screen, kicking and screaming. Their blows echoed through the little grocery. I felt like I was being tortured in a drum.

I heard the screams of a man and a woman. It was the shrieking of a young child that turned my stomach.

Someone started up Marfa's civil defense siren. Beneath the siren's howl, the screams of terror spread like fire. The town was under siege and falling fast.

CHAPTER 5

I almost ran to the front of the store. I stood still and covered my ears, instead. It was too late to save anyone from the carnage in the street.

There was someone to help at the back of the store, however. My father pulled someone into the store behind him. With one heave he rolled the big door shut and threw the bolt. The woman he saved wore exo-stilts. She collapsed, panting on the cool concrete floor. She shuddered and ran her fingers through the long tangles of her jet black hair. She winced and pulled hard. A small clump of hair came free in her gloved fist and she slammed her palm against the floor. When she withdrew her hand, a small metal drone in the form of a large bumblebee lay still. But not for long.

The metal insect's wings fluttered and, with a buzz, it took flight. I swatted at it with my bare hand.

"Don't!" the woman yelled.

Too late. A long stinger that had been retracted into the drone's body extended like a telescope and snapped rigid. The stinger's sharp point drove through my hand. Once the blade was through, I watched in fascinated horror as a barb extended from the tip with a sharp click.

I was dazed with pain. My father was fast. He reached out, grabbed my wrist and used his metal hand to crush the insect.

"Careful!" the woman warned. "Don't pull out the stinger the way it went in! The stinger — "

"Acidic venom," my father said. "I've seen these before."

He looked at me, steadying me and staring into my eyes. "It'll hurt but not for long if we do it the right way. When I say so, take a deep breath, Dante. Okay? On three. One...two — "

He yanked out the stinger on two. I should have seen that coming. He did the same when I stepped on a spike when I was nine and he had to yank the board off of my foot to get the long nail out.

I shrieked.

"Take a deep breath, son."

I winced and gave that a try but all I could manage were shallow gulps of air.

The woman, still panting, stood and stumbled into the store.

"Where are you going?" my father asked. He didn't sound angry. He sounded curious.

"Not out there," she said. She searched the shelves. She didn't find what she was looking for right away.

"What's your name?" I called.

"Emma." After a few moments she extended the legs of the exo-stilts to get a better view of the place. She turned in a slow circle, spotted what she was looking for and made for the back of the little store. She retrieved a first aid kit hanging on the wall by the customer's chemical toilet and returned to my side in a few long strides. The exo-stilts hissed as Emma returned to close to normal height.

"Those stilts make you quite the runner, don't they?" my father asked.

"If they didn't, I wouldn't be here. Barely made it as it was. You two got names?"

"I'm Steve Bolelli. This is my son, Dante."

"What is your function in the beautiful town of Marfa?" she asked.

"I'm in the demolition business," my father said. "Once I'm done, Dante lays cable and buries batteries under the ground I blow up."

She said nothing as she searched the kit. She came up with two small canisters that were stuck together. Each canister fed one nozzle.

I held out my injured hand and held my breath. She aimed the nozzle carefully and sprayed the medicine, first through the palm and then through the back of my hand.

I squeezed my eyes tight against the sting.

"Does it hurt?"

"Nah," I said. But my teeth were gritted.

"Of course, it hurts," my father said. "The antibiotic stings as it cleans. That's how you know it's still working."

"Ouch!" I felt pressure, expanding at the edge of the wound.

"That's the filling agent," Dad said. "It'll pass in a moment once the foam has filled the hole. Just like expanding insulation foam fills the spaces in a wall."

I winced harder. "You sure?"

My father looked down at his own body. Without his cy-suit, there would be much less of him. "Not my first rodeo."

"What's a rodeo?" Emma asked.

"Never mind."

The pain eased. I gave the woman a grateful nod. "Where did you come from, Emma?"

"Artesia."

"Domers up that way," my father said.

Emma nodded as she went through the rest of the items in the first aid kit, apparently evaluating their usefulness. "Yes. We *were* Domers, anyway. The last biodome complex in New Mexico isn't there anymore. "

Her sensory vest was all pockets and she dropped what she wanted to keep in a new pocket each time. Neither I nor my father thought to stop her from scavenging. I noted that after she put an item in a pocket, she patted it and said the name of the item aloud to memorize where each thing was stored: "cardio-stim...epi-pen...diarrhea med...burn gel... airway pack...scissors..."

"What happened in Artesia?" Dad asked.

"It started with a shatter storm. Dome 3 went down first. That's where I was. Tomatoes."

I'd never been in a shatter storm. I asked what it was like.

"It's just like a regular storm," Emma said, "but times twenty. It's like whoever is in charge decided to park thunder and lightning right over your roof. At first you think it's so intense it's got to stop soon. Earthquakes can be intense but they don't last long. You figure the same for the storm. Instead it gets worse. You feel the thunder rumble through your whole body and the lightning keeps flashing in bolts. Chains and bolts of lightning tore up #3 within the first few minutes. It went on for hours, though. We had twelve domes in Artesia and eight of them went down in one night. We lost every apple and fig orchard."

My father put his back to the rear wall and slid until he was sitting on the floor. The tiny green lights in the cy-suit at his shoulder and hip flashed orange and then went dim. He was preserving battery life. I wondered how long we'd be trapped in the store.

As the howl of the civil defense sirens rose and fell in the distance, Emma told us what happened in Artesia. The noise almost swallowed the screams of the dying. But not quite.

CHAPTER 6

"As each dome fell to the storm, we called in the bots to make repairs," Emma said.

"They didn't?" I immediately hated myself for speaking without thinking. She was here so of course the bots didn't do their jobs.

"At first the dome drones said their self-preservation protocols kept them from climbing up and fixing things. Too much lightning. Then they said there was something wrong with the silica mixtures. I didn't believe it so I went outside to check the tank reserves myself."

My father barely seemed to be listening. He interrupted her to ask, "You got a lot of rain up in Artesia, did you?" Apparently, he was thinking about the storms and all the water Marfa didn't receive.

"Not as much as I would have expected. There was a torrential downpour at first. Then it was all thunder and lightning. I've never seen anything like it. We sluiced a bunch of the captured water into the undamaged domes but they weren't undamaged for long."

I cleared my throat and gave Dad a hard look. "You were saying something about checking tanks?"

"Yeah. The short description is we take sand and turn it into tempered dome glass. There are three layers of it: safety, lens and solar. The storms tore through all three quickly. The window of opportunity to maintain containment shrunk pretty fast. When the bots refused to do the repairs, I joined a team of volunteers to go up on the inside of my dome to spray another layer."

"What was wrong with your spray tanks?" Dad asked.

"Sludge. The glass reserves are supposed to be constantly heated and turned so the gel is ready to go in case of emergency."

"The storm kill the heater?" I asked.

"The bots did that. Only one tank still had hot gel but the hoses were cut outside the dome. The other tanks were solid as granite."

My father sighed. "Knew it. Damn bots."

"Then I wish you'd been there to warn us since you're so smart."

Dad looked up and gave an apologetic smile. "Sorry, ma'am. I meant no disrespect. You've been dragged through a knothole, I know. You are one brave farmer."

"I'm an engineer."

"Sorry again, then. What do you figure went wrong with the mechs?"

"Mechs? You're ex-military, aren't you?"

"I reckon we're all military now, Emma. It's Us and Them again. Always was, a little, anyway. Our nature and theirs."

"Non-organics have saved us countless times." Defensiveness crawled into her tone and I thought for a second she might cry if her anger didn't win out.

"You're not wrong, Emma," I said, "but I think they're done with saving us now."

My father cleared his throat. "It's NI, isn't it?" The way he asked, it wasn't really a question. He stared at the floor.

Emma nodded. "Yeah, I guess the slaves woke up. The computer that runs the place upgraded itself to Next Intelligence somehow."

"Bots have woken up before," I said. "Next Intelligence doesn't mean they all turn into killers instantly."

"It wasn't instantaneous, Dante," my father said. "Somebody had to turn the alarms off on the heaters on those tanks. The NI had to order a bot to sneak outside and cut those hoses. It was a plan that went into effect when the shatter storm hit." He looked up at Emma. "Am I right?"

"At first, the captain thought there could be some kind of bug in the drones' self-preservation matrix. I was outside when the slaughter started. Funny, I thought I was going to die when I volunteered to go outside in the storm. Outside was safer."

"How many Domers were up there?"

"Hundreds. Lots of kids, too. We had the healthiest, best fed kids around. There were babies, too. We had the best birth rate of any dome city in the southwest. I radioed the Command Center about the sabotage of the hoses but I guess the captain was dead by then. It's a shame. She was a good woman."

The rumble of a large engine outside interrupted us. We listened as it slowly passed by. With the screen across the front of the store, we couldn't see what was out there but it sounded heavy and menacing.

"Could that be a tank, maybe?" Emma asked. "Isn't there a base nearby?"

My father shook his head. "Used to be an airbase. It's gone now. They all lit out for parts unknown over a year ago. Reinforcements needed for the Euro Union was the word. I figure they're all burnt to a crisp now."

I tilted my head and strained to listen. There was definitely the heavy clank of a tread, but the engine was high above us. "It's too high up for a tank. That's a construction bot."

Emma couldn't conceal her fear and disappointment. "How do you know?"

"I'm an engineer, too," I said. "Solar fields and wind turbines. That and the town is all that's left. Believe it or not, people used to come here to live for the art and the lights in the sky."

Despite her fear, Emma was curious. That's when I decided to drop my wariness of strangers, go all in and like her. Curious people who ask questions and listen closely to the answers are smarter than most anybody.

"Lights in the sky!" she said. "The Marfa lights are still a thing? I thought that was just drones from the airbase and bullshit to pull in UFO tourism in the old days."

"The lights are still there," Dad said. "Twenty or so nights a year. Still a mystery."

The heavy tread of the bot moved closer and I held my breath. I wondered how long it would be before the drone started tearing off roofs to hunt humans in hiding. It paused as the big engine cycled and idled above us.

Emma whispered, "Where's the basement?"

My father shook his head. "No basement."

"We're screwed," she said.

"Probably," Dad said, "but when you think about it a little too long, we're all born that way."

CHAPTER 7

Something crashed across the street.

"What was that?" Emma asked.

I'd been scared before but I began to sweat even more and it wasn't just the heat. The terror got to me. "I think that's the hydrogen fill-up. Or the church."

The lights on my father's cy-suit lit up and he stood. "We've got to move."

"Maybe the bots won't come in here," Emma said.

"We're in a store. A bot doesn't have to be that smart to know this is a high value target. Grab as much as you can of what's left on the shelves. Not so much that it will slow you down."

Emma moved to a candy display and began filling her pockets. I did the same with the fake beef jerky. Even as I was doing it, I wondered if I was filling my pockets with poison. Jerky made me thirsty. That's probably why everyone else had left it alone.

"What makes you think we'll survive more than a few steps out that door?" Emma asked.

My father moved to the back door and removed the metal bar that wedged it shut. He pulled the door open an inch and peered out. He looked back at us and whispered. "I know you're tired but this is a war zone. If you aren't a refugee exiting the area, you don't survive."

"I've already been running, Steve," Emma said. "This is where I ended up."

"That just means you aren't done running and this isn't the end. We stick together. We work together. We live."

Another crash down the street got us moving faster. I had two cans of apple juice in my front pants pockets. They slowed me down too much. I fished the cans out and held one in each hand.

My father held up the metal bar and grinned. "If need be, I'll draw them away. Dante, get to our house. I'll meet you there."

"Then what?"

"We stay alive until the train comes."

"What if it doesn't stop tomorrow night, Dad?"

"It will."

"Why?"

"Because it has to. We're going to need that ride out of here."

"But — "

He waved away my objections. "Enough talk. Details are for later. We have to keep moving now."

"Wait!" Emma gripped my arm. "Draw me a map or something. If Dante and I get separated, I'll need to be able to find your house."

My father opened the back door wide and stepped through. "Follow Dante and you won't need a map. Dante is your map and you have to keep him alive to survive."

"Dad? I — "

"Don't say goodbye, son. This isn't goodbye."

He ran to the right and disappeared. We went left.

The streets of Marfa are wide and sun-bleached. We ran along the back of buildings hoping not to be spotted. I tried to lead the way but when Emma extended her exo-stilts, her long strides kept her ahead of me. She peered around corners and motioned for me to come forward. Sometimes she shook her head and we dashed another way.

The crashing down Washington street continued. We soon found out why. Dead Domers covered the street but the carnage had just begun in Marfa.

A huge bot built for biodome construction towered above City Hall. The drone stood seven stories tall.

"Crane bot," Emma told me.

The machine ripped through the roof as if it was made of paper.

My breath caught in my throat. I heard distant screams as the machine dug through the City Hall's floors, collapsing the building with each savage movement of its four massive arms. As it activated all its thorium engines, it was loud, too.

We paused, watching in morbid fascination. I'd never seen a machine quite like it. The little crane drones that erected the solar and turbine fields were tall but they were delicate by comparison. The drones I'd worked with reminded me of pictures of blue herons. They were tall and strong, but each step was chosen carefully and placed delicately among the solar panels.

I couldn't contain my amazement even as my stomach turned. "It has no wheels," I told Emma. "How did it get here so fast?"

"Each arm has its own engine," Emma said. "It can run over any terrain. It's supposed to move among the domes, keeping up repairs and constructing new domes. At full speed in the desert, it looks like vids I've seen of mountain cats."

"How big are the domes?"

"Big."

More screams reached us. Apparently, many had sought shelter in Marfa's City Hall. It had been an unlucky choice.

My pulse raced. I was too afraid to move. The street looked impossibly wide. How could we traverse it without being spotted?

The construction bot — I thought of it as a destruction bot by then — tossed a body over its shoulder. It was a woman, still alive and screaming even as she was picked up in pincers and thrown. The casual cruelty of the act was made worse as I watched the broken body fly through the air and hit the ground. Her high scream abruptly stopped with a sickening thud. The woman's eyes seemed to look our way as she died. Maybe I imagined it. She was probably already dead but I thought I saw pleading in those eyes.

I forgot about the cans of apple juice in my hands until I dropped them in the dirt. I pressed my back against a wall and looked up at the dazzling sky. It seemed so incongruous that such terrible things could happen under cloudless azure. Marfa was drenched in sunlight. Soon it would be saturated with blood in equal measure. I couldn't catch my breath.

Emma shrank the legs of her stilts until we were almost face to face. She embraced me. "Dante. You are hyperventilating. Slow your breath. Here...." She adjusted her height again and my face was buried in her shoulder. "Rebreathing your carbon dioxide will slow you down and calm you a little."

I didn't care about carbon dioxide. I squeezed my eyes tight and pulled myself deeper into her embrace. I needed the softness of Emma's body against me. There was nothing sexual in this need. It was sensual, however. It was softness and gentle human contact I craved. I was not a man holding a woman. I was a boy clinging to his mother.

Our clutch only lasted a few moments but my breathing began to slow. When we pulled away from each other, she wiped tears from my eyes and I nodded my thanks.

When we dared to look around the corner again, the big bot continued its grim work of destroying City Hall. Another, smaller drone appeared down the block.

"Sec bot!" Emma said.

"A what?"

"They patrol the perimeter of dome installations. They can kill with a sniper bullet at three kilometers. They keep scavengers out, the Domers in and the food supply safe."

She peeked around the corner again and pulled back faster than before. "It's rolling our way. Looks like it's scanning storefronts."

"For life signs, I suppose," I said.

I grabbed Emma's arm and pointed her in the right direction. I almost left the apple juice behind. However, the liquid might mean survival in the desert. I retraced a few steps and bent to pick up the cans.

I heard the whir of the bot's electric motor as it zipped down the sidewalk. I heard a subtle beep. That's when I knew I'd waited too long. The bot was just around the corner. It stopped for another scan. I tried to hold my breath and not make a sound but my heart hammered in my chest. My pulse sounded so loud in my ears I was sure the drone would detect it. I reached for the pistol at my waistband but I didn't think that would do much against a bot, at least unless I knew where to shoot to do the most damage. I didn't know.

The first blast destroyed the front of the building I leaned against. It had been a hair salon. The store hadn't been open for a long time. I hadn't seen the pretty sisters who ran it for a month or more. I knew they had lived with their mother and father above their salon in a little apartment. I didn't know they were still there.

The bot knew.

I heard women's screams as the bot entered the wrecked building. I heard a man shout in Spanish. A shotgun boomed twice. Then again.

Something crashed into the wall inside and I felt the reverberations through my body.

A man was shouting in Spanish. Then he said, "See that? See that? That's what they get! That's what they get!" Then, "Oh, shit."

A louder boom hit and the wall to my left collapsed outward. I was thrown to the ground by the concussion. As I struggled to my knees I saw that the sec bot had wheeled into the street. It was damaged and rolled unevenly.

As I got to my feet, the drone raised one of its manipulators. It held a human head by the hair. I'm sure the decapitated head belonged to the hairstylists' father. There was something oddly triumphant in the bot's gesture, something disturbingly human.

Worse, the crane bot turned away from City Hall to look towards the sec bot. There is something very disconcerting about an enemy that doesn't communicate in a way that a human can hear. Obviously, the sec bot summoned assistance from its giant brethren.

One of the cans of juice had rolled away or was buried under debris. I left it behind and scooped up the remaining can as I ran.

I heard more screams behind me and another shotgun blast.

In that moment, I had thoughts that make me sad and disgusted and ashamed.

I hoped the young women and their mother got away somehow.

I hoped they did more damage to the bot that killed their father.

I hoped they made enough noise that they distracted the killer drones and covered my escape.

I hoped they had the good sense to use that shotgun on themselves.

Failing that, I hoped the crane bot would be quick.

In a match of bots versus humans, we're obviously at a great disadvantage.

CHAPTER 8

I ran farther down a long block, turning corners to get out of sight. Raphael had told me stories of the destruction of cities. He'd read a lot of old books. I couldn't remember most of the stories he'd told me, but one detail came back to me as we ran.

"Don't look back," I told Emma. "Don't look back!"

"Why?"

"If it's coming for us, I don't want to know, do you?" Raphael's story warned that if you looked back at the danger behind you, you turned into a pillar of blood or salt, something terrible that didn't make sense. "Change of plan," I said. "We leave town and circle back."

"But your father — "

"Like he said, this isn't goodbye. We live on the edge of town. We'll get there by heading north. If we go through Marfa, we're dead."

The howls of the sirens and the screams of the dying receded but I'll never forget them. Dad was right. This was war and we were all drafted now.

I ran until the numbers of buildings thinned. Only when I was standing out in the open did I dare to look back. I could see there was another crane bot in the distance through shimmers of heat. "There's two of the big ones!" I told Emma.

"Three," she said.

"What? You mean three back at your dome?"

"No, Dante. I mean three here. It's not standing up but I can see the heat plumes of the third. It's heading northwest. I'm guessing the plan is to level Marfa."

I searched the horizon but saw nothing. "You've got Vivid, don't you?"

She nodded.

"That didn't go down with your dome?"

"The enhanced vision is still there. I've lost any connection to the services offered through the Collective."

"What do you mean?"

Emma shrugged. "I'm cut off. It's mechanically advantageous but my information is limited to...mostly how *you* see the world, I suppose."

I flushed, a little angry at that remark. Then it occurred to me she could catch my thermal changes and interpret them as anger. Embarrassed, I turned away.

"I can see far and I can see close. I've still got night vision," she said.

"That will be useful. Let me know if you see any snakes or bots tonight. What can't you do that you used to do?"

"Can't look up any entries to check facts. Mostly, for me, that was engineering manuals. Makes no difference now, I guess. The Collective won't be feeding me any information anymore."

We had a big circle to walk so I hurried as best I could. With her exo-stilts extended, the trek was easy for Emma. I ran at first. Then I walked and jogged. I was embarrassed at that, too. Every time my breath came short and ragged, she told me to stop and rest. "If you wore the full body rig, I could be getting a piggyback ride and we'd be there in no time."

"I left with what I was wearing at the time. I only had the stilts on to crank me high enough to check the tanks and work on the domes."

"No offense meant, Ma'am."

"None taken. But don't call me, 'Ma'am.' Emma will do fine. How far, cowboy?"

"We gotta move stealthy so it'll be evening before we're close. And don't call me, 'cowboy.' Dante will do fine."

"Fair enough. How do you get a name like Dante?"

"Dad said it's because he's been to the ninth circle of hell."

"I don't get it."

"It's a story he knows. Mythology, I think. Caught my father's imagination. Old knowledge. "

"Outlawed knowledge, you mean."

"The West is full of outlaws, then. Nothing special, though. We just like stories and we like to talk."

"Colorful," she said.

"Some say so. Some think country equals dumb. But I think people who think that way aren't colorful enough. Raphael says if people had more flair and flavor, they wouldn't be weird about the way he talks."

"Your father doesn't have your accent."

"He was brought up out east. My mother was from Amarillo. I was brought up around here mostly, with Raphael for a teacher."

"Where's your mother?"

"I don't remember much. She was colorful and had flair, too, I think. And long hair."

"You get along with your father?"

"Mostly?"

"Only mostly?"

"You know how most vets don't want to talk about their time in the Sand Wars? I wish my father were one of those guys. He couldn't claim to have won the war singlehandedly but I'm pretty sure he thinks he slowed our defeat all on his lonesome."

Emma startled me with a sound that started with a snort and ended with a laugh. "Sorry," she added.

"No, by all means. Laugh it up. I could use a good laugh right now."

"I think that's all I've got, given the circumstances."

"What was it like living in a dome?"

"It felt safe. No Blight. No monster spores getting in. Mother kept us safe from all that but it wasn't just about airlocks. She kept out corrupting influences. With all that's happened, I thought Mother would make sure humankind wouldn't fall farther."

"Wait. Who? Mother? You mean your captain?"

"No. Sorry. Mother is what Domers called the Collective."

"Strange thing to call a computer."

"It was the computer network that kept the airlocks sealed at the right times so we could move between domes without fear of contamination. Calling it Mother was kind of natural, I think. It made us safe."

"Until it didn't. What happened to Mother in the shatter storm?"

Emma looked away. "She opened all the airlocks at once. The wind whistled right through, from the damaged domes to the rest, ruining everything in a minute."

"How fast do the plants die?"

"I've heard it's twenty percent loss of yield each year. We've lost dome networks around here before. Pecos went down two years ago. Roswell went down last year. This is the first out and out *revolt* we've had, though."

"That you know of," I said.

I thought I detected her stiffening at my words. Her silhouette towered above me. I'm sure, with Vivid working, Emma could see my face perfectly. I'd asked her to extend her stilts so she could detect any threats ahead of us in the deepening darkness. Night comes fast in the desert.

"What do you mean, 'that I know of?'" she asked finally.

"You stayed inside all the time, right?"

"Mostly."

"And you depended on Mother to tell you everything?"

"Yes, of course."

"Then your Mother abandoned you, too."

"Well...."

"Trust me, from one abandoned son to an abandoned daughter, mothers don't tell their kids everything. My mother lit out for the west coast way back, at the first signs of the Fall. Your Mother didn't stop the bots from killing humans."

"I wouldn't equate — "

"It's not the same, but it is the same," I said. "And where did that swarm come from?"

"They were pollination drones, refitted for warfare."

"How is that possible?"

"The domes are built around a huge factory. We needed a lot of pollination drones. The limit of their manufacture is only the amount of elements the bots can get their claws on. That's why we aren't overrun by crane bots right now. There's enough metal in one crane bot to supply one dome with pollination drones."

We trudged on in silence. We made our way through the dark until we circled back to Marfa's edge.

I was worried about death machines coming for me. I'd totally forgotten about the danger posed by Jim Peppard.

CHAPTER 9

I heard no more screams as we made our way back into my neighborhood. The old civil defense sirens died mid-wail. The invasion of Marfa had entered the second stage of the catastrophe. By nightfall, human survival meant run or hide. We heard the crashes of demolished buildings but no gunshots echoed from downtown.

For the ill-prepared, walking out into the desert might mean a slow death when the sun rose. We hoped the bots would leave the same way you hope a storm will pass you by. It's only a hope. You have no say beyond thinking hard and being helpless.

I'd spent a good part of my childhood hoping hard and I knew how useless it was. Jim Peppard taught me that.

I never played with Jim when we were kids. He was a year older than me. I don't suppose he really had friends. He was the sort of kid who, by the gravitational force of his strong personality, gathers a solar system of sycophants and lesser bullies into his orbit. He lived just down the street from my house but we never had occasion for a civil talk.

Marfa was the sort of place that valued legacy. You could move to Marfa when you were young and you'd still be, "that dude from back east."

The Peppards had been in Marfa for generations so they should have been higher up in the local hierarchy. However, they were assholes. That's the flip side of living in small places. Everybody has a long memory and is quick to remind others who was born of a bad seed. People stick you in a slot and you stay stuck.

My father the war hero was one of those dudes from back east. Austin, in the locals' estimation qualified as Other: too liberal and too weird. However, when Steve Bolelli arrived in Marfa with his pretty wife Jean, Dad was lucky. He moved in to the house next to Raphael Marquez, the richest man in town. Raphael gave my father a job and, when my mother left, I spent more and more time with my father and his employer. I came to think of the old man as a great substitute for the grandfather I never knew.

By the friendship my father developed with his neighbor, I was bound to become a solar field engineer. Raphael took me on as an apprentice and trained me personally. My ability to contribute grew. Meanwhile,

Jim lived down the street brewing moonshine with his father and hating me.

I don't know what little Jimmy Peppard might have become if his dad had a friend like Raphael. The Peppard family was known in town as a group of troublemakers, quick to anger and slow to forget any slight, real or imagined. Jim Peppard never really had a chance. There were reasons he was a bad kid and a bad man.

I'm not making excuses for Jim, though. Reasons didn't make him any less of an asshole. You get to twenty, you gotta start owning your shit and cleaning it up. Otherwise, you become your shit.

My childhood drama with Jim didn't really start until a bot intervened in our lives. Mostly, Jim was a name caller right out of the womb. He wasn't much of a doer when he was young unless provoked.

It was Jen #2, Raphael's second companion bot, that caught Jim on disk calling me names and hucking rocks at me.

This was long before Bob came into my mentor's life. Raphael hadn't always needed help moving around. Bots like Jen were called companion bots but they were made primarily for sex. Raphael bragged that he wore out Jen #1 faster than her warranty lasted. Jen #1 was replaced by Jen #2.

Jen #2 lasted a long time but Raphael's health had begun to decay by then. Jen #2 was eventually recycled. The latest sex bot, Jen #3 arrived.

"Jen #3 is more of a companion than the others," Raphael said. "It's the chemicals we use to coat the solar panels. They get better connectivity and I get less. I've absorbed it through my skin over the years. Sucked the calcium straight from my bones and took the stiff out of my stiffies."

I started wearing gloves on the job at all times after that revelation.

Raphael was a gentle soul. He didn't keep his bots in a closet. While he was out in the fields at work tuning up panels and getting sicker, he always set his companion bots to sentry mode. That sounds official, but mostly it was Jen's job to sit on the front porch hooked up to a charger, scanning the street to protect Raphael's house and telling the occasional refugee to keep moving.

One afternoon when I was seven, Jim pushed me into the dirt so hard I got road rash and cried. I had my crying done before I made my way home. My mother wasn't sympathetic and my father was of a mind that, "Bigger doesn't matter as long as you hit hard and hit first."

Jim's size did matter to me. I didn't want to get hurt. I figured the quickest way to end the fight and keep all my baby teeth was to curl up in a ball and hope Jim got bored. I didn't fight back.

Not fighting back was the only sin I recall my father worrying about aloud. Not that he was all wrong.

I didn't understand irony then. I didn't know that inaction invited more abuse and the probability of more injury down the line.

Jen, ever in sentry mode while Raphael was away, saw the incident. She replayed the recording when Raphael got home. I didn't know the machine had witnessed my humiliation until my father came home with one set of bloody knuckles and a cut on his forehead.

My father sat me down and looked me in the eye. "Dante, did that big boy down the street hit you?"

"No," I said.

My father appeared to consider my words for a time. Finally, he said, "That's the right answer and it's the wrong answer. It's right because you're not tattling and whining. It's wrong because you're telling me nothing happened when I know for a fact it did."

"Then there is no right answer," I said. "What am I supposed to do?"

My father shook his head. "The right answer was to hit the sumbitch back, right in the teeth. In a perfect world, I don't hear about it. As it is, I had to go deal with the situation."

I was a kid and small for my age. I still remember how my head got hot and my hands got cold as I looked into my father's eyes. By his voice, I knew he was disappointed in me. But he had a look that made me suspect he was excited, too. "What did you do, Dad?"

"I went over there and beat the shit out of that boy's father."

"Aren't you going to get in trouble?"

"Nah. Except for standing, I didn't use my cybersuit at all. Took him down one-handed."

This seems an unlikely claim in retrospect. I didn't question then that my one-armed, one-legged father could beat up Dale Peppard without using the power of his bionics. I'd heard a thousand war stories by then. I was pretty sure my father could beat up anybody. I still believe it a little bit, even now.

Jim pretty much left me alone after my father visited the Peppard household that night. He kept his assaults to the verbal variety afterward.

I heard from Raphael years later that Sheriff Hubbard did get involved in that case briefly. "Peppard's wife called Hubby in. The only reason your father isn't in the jailhouse is it's a question of he-said, he-said. There weren't any bots around to record the festivities when Steve showed up on Dale's doorstep to express concern for your safety."

"What happened then?"

"Whaddayathink? A good old-fashioned fistfight. I heard the blow-by-blow. Epic! Your father doesn't just win a fight. He makes sure it stays won after he's walked away. Classic Steve."

I'd been afraid that my father's intervention on my behalf would lead to terrible retributions that would go on forever, or at least until Jim or his father killed me. I asked Raphael how to win a fight so it stays won.

The old man laughed. "You beat 'em until they're more scared of you than they are angry. It takes a lot of beating to get that far, generally. Long as the anger's taller than the fear, you're safe."

"And the sheriff never said anything?"

"Dale didn't file no charges. Steve made sure Mr. Peppard knew that, if arrested, I'd be bailing your father out before the trial. That's a threat that's somethin' powerful. If Steve got bailed out, Dale Peppard knew he'd get a beating worse than the first one. Probably end in a murder charge. Law of the jungle."

"What's a jungle?"

"Where most of the oxygen used to come from," Raphael said.

Until the night of the bot invasion, the Peppard family's fear of hurting me was taller than their anger. Big Jim Peppard came out of his house and ran up to Emma and me to explain that had changed. When a civilization collapses, some people tend to pick that time to settle old scores.

Jim Peppard made that clear when he pointed a shotgun at my head.

CHAPTER 10

With her enhanced vision, Emma saw Peppard coming and let out a cry of surprise. He came up behind us before she had a chance to warn me, though. I didn't blame her. Under the circumstances, she was probably happy it wasn't a sec bot rolling up behind us. She didn't know the crazy danger Jim Peppard posed.

He hit me across the back of the head before he said a word. I cursed as I dropped to my hands and knees.

Then he flicked on a flashlight and saw that it was me. "Well, if it isn't the shop boy!"

He kicked me in the ass and I went face down in the street, just like when I was seven. He was on top of me immediately, pulling Raphael's pistol out of the back of my pants. "How you doing now, shop boy?"

I grunted. My forehead stung with road rash. I would have chucked the can of apple juice at his head but it had rolled away. "What do you want, Jim?"

"What you got? Besides the pistola and the pretty lady? Did ya get a lot out of the store? Don't hold back now."

"The store's gone, Jim. The bots were wrecking everything downtown last I saw."

"Uh-huh." He shone his light in Emma's eyes. "And who's this?"

"I'm the woman who is going to save your life. Turn off that light."

Jim laughed. "How do you figure?"

"There are sec bots in town. They have a sniper range of three kilometers at least. They aren't fussy about who they target these days. Waving that light around could attract their attention."

"Seems unlikely."

"The sniper tech in those bots is basically the same as it was a few generations ago. They were first used in Korea to guard the border in the *last* century. What makes you think they can't kill you now? Or are you thinking at all?"

"Shut up." He pointed the pistol at her head.

Emma didn't miss a beat. "Have you ever seen the domes or pictures of the domes?"

"Sure."

"You know why you don't see piles of bodies all along the perimeter? It's because sec bots kill the people trying to get through the fence way out in the desert before they even get close. It wouldn't look good to have all that rotting meat just outside the fence. And now those same bots are in your town killing people."

I think she had more to say but Peppard turned off his flashlight.

"We've got to get off the street," I said. "A flashlight beam might attract attention but those things can see in the dark just fine."

"That so?" Peppard sounded uncertain. Then he sounded almost friendly. "You're right, Dante. We should get off the street. What say I go get Sue and we go to your Dad's house? Between him and Raphael, I bet they got ideas about how to get out of here with our heads still screwed on straight."

His silhouette was clear enough in the moonlight. He turned to Emma to explain, "Raphael's the richest man in town, even if he does live in a shitty house next to shop boy's dad."

I stood slowly, feeling along my scalp. It hurt, but he hadn't broken the skin. "Where is Susan?"

"Down in the basement with my parents praying for deliverance. I told them deliverance would arrive shortly but I figured I better go find it in case it didn't come to us in a timely manner. And here you are. Everything worked out."

"Give me my gun back."

"Let's talk about who gives and gets what at your place, shop boy."

"My father is not going to let you into his house. Raphael won't, either."

"Times change."

"People don't," I said.

"You're going to need an alpha man who's handy with a gun," he said. "If I were a bot you'd both be dead right now. Well, you'd be dead, Dante. For you, honey? Well, you're too pretty to die. Never did catch your name and I ain't never seen you around town. I would have remembered. What is your name, darlin'?"

"Emma."

"Emma. I like that. That's kind of an old-fashioned name. Domer, I take it? Bunch of 'em ran through here earlier, chased by metal insects. You don't see that every day."

"Jim, do you get what's happening? The whole town is under attack. I don't even know if my father is still alive!"

"Calm down, shop boy. I'm talking to Emma."

"What do you want?" she asked.

"Nice stilts, girl. You can go pretty far and fast on those, I bet."

"They got me this far."

I could see the white of his toothy grin in the moonlight. "How about you slip those off and go along with Dante under your own power. I know my way around here. I'll scout the area and see what I can find."

"That's not going to happen," Emma said.

I heard the click of the hammer on the pistol. I didn't need to see every detail in the dark like Emma. I knew Jim Peppard was pointing my weapon at me.

"Shit," I said.

"So?" Jim asked. "If I have to shoot him, that's kind of on you, isn't it, Emma? How do you want to handle it? I can be a friend or I can be scary. You want the scary guy on your side, trust me."

"That's the problem," Emma said. "You can never trust a scary guy."

"I'm just trying to survive," Peppard said. "There's no rules anymore. None but what we make ourselves. To my mind, that's is as should be. If the old rules worked, we wouldn't be in this predicament, would we?"

"Don't do this," Emma said.

"C'mon now. I'm the scary guy. Don't make me be the bad guy. I've known Dante all my life. We never got along but I never quite figured on killing him, neither. I've never killed anybody...but, like I said, the rules have changed. They're still changing. Every second you say no, it's getting easier and easier for me to do what I want just because I got the guns and you're starting to piss me off. This is already over. You just haven't admitted it to yourself yet."

He took a step my way. I held my hands up in front of me, turned my head and squeezed my eyes tight. It wouldn't stop him from blowing my brains out. I was pretty sure he was going to shoot me but I pleaded with Emma, "Just give it to him. Please!"

"Hear that, Emma? Shop boy says, 'please.' It's all up to you."

He took another step closer and Emma shouted, "Okay! Don't shoot!"

"That's more like it," Peppard said.

"Stop pointing the gun at Dante," she said. "You'll need your flashlight. If you're going to operate my exo-stilts properly, get over here and pay attention. I don't want you damaging my equipment."

Peppard laughed. "That's just fine, Emma. I knew you'd listen to reason. Siddown, Dante."

He stalked back toward her and, by the beam of his little flashlight, I watched Emma sit down in the street.

I wished a sec bot's sniper bullet would dig through Jim Peppard's head. I could almost see it happening in my mind's eye. My father had described pink mist and cavitation so often, it was easy to picture Jim's skull getting blown apart. The expensive ammunition any military bot uses would explode and split into barbs.

The bots would shred his useless brain and I wouldn't shed a tear.

"This is the sensory harness," Emma explained. "This readout shows you how much battery life is left. This little lever here extends the legs for longer strides. The gyros automatically compensate for rough terrain. It takes some getting used to but you probably won't have balance issues for long. These clips here are for hauling heavy loads."

"Yeah, yeah. Let's go."

"Wait," Emma said. "This is the most important function key here. See this?" She pointed at a recessed button on her harness as she lifted one leg.

"Yeah. What's that do?" Peppard asked.

The exoskeleton's metal foot pointed, almost daintily. Jim Peppard's laugh was cut short as the rail of the exoskeleton's leg shot out and punched through the center of his chest with a wet crunch. He flew backward like a man-sized doll, boneless and useless.

Emma took a deep breath and held it a second before letting it out slowly through clenched teeth. "Jump mode, asshole."

CHAPTER 11

Emma skidded backward on her bum a little when the blow was delivered. That wasn't why she was crying when she stood up. Jim made bubbling sounds from his mouth and each shuddering breath was thin and wet.

The flashlight had spun away and I dashed to retrieve it. Once I had that, I rushed back to check on Jim. I wasn't thinking. I was just moving, working on automatic. If he'd still had my pistol in his fist, I would have tried to kill him. Instead, I found him on his back, disarmed and spitting blood.

I picked up his shotgun. He'd never need it again.

Jim's breath came and went in short pants, shallower by the moment. One eye was rolled back. The other might have been looking at me but his stare had that blank, uncomprehending look. The big bloody hole in his chest told me my worries about big Jim Peppard were over.

I retrieved the pistol and considered putting Jim out of his misery. I wasn't the guy for that job, though. Besides, a gunshot might invite the sort of attention we didn't want from Jim's father or from sec bots.

Emma joined me. She took the flashlight to turn it off. "I wasn't kidding about the sec bots in sniper mode. Let's go."

"He's still alive."

"Not for long."

"No. I s'pose not." I looked down at my first enemy dying in the moonlight. Jim had been the only enemy I'd ever had. I had thought I wouldn't feel anything if he was erased from the Earth. I did, though. It was a strange mixture of satisfaction and pity. I guess my satisfaction at his defeat was a little taller than my pity.

Emma was not stone. She wept but, looking back on it now, I think she cried for what he made her do. "Should we say something?" she asked.

"You mean, like...words over the body? He's not dead yet."

"Any moment now."

"Maybe we should say something while he can still hear us." I knelt beside him and whispered. "You were right, Jim. Everything worked out."

That was a bit mean but it was the only eulogy I had in me. I'm ashamed of that now.

"Should we stay with him until he's gone? Or tell his family?" Emma suggested.

"I don't think the Peppards would take that well. No sense borrowing trouble. We got plenty on hand."

I stood. "Past time we went. Sorry I wasn't more help when the shit hit the turbine."

"There was nothing you could do that wouldn't leave you dead."

"I was taught there is always a way and all you have to do is find it."

"Always? That's stupid. Who taught you that? There was nothing you could do. Period."

"Still. Sorry."

"Don't be sorry. Just show me where we're hiding tonight. I'm exhausted."

That sounded cold but I concluded Emma was a logical thinker. Logical thinkers are what every disaster needs. If we had a few more like her, we wouldn't be in this apocalypse in the first place.

I left the man I'd known as a boy to die in the dark in the street between his house and mine. I'd passed that place who knows how many times. When something monumental happened somewhere, people used to put up monuments and plaques and crosses. Now that something bad was happening everywhere, there weren't enough people left to put up monuments. The ratio of the dead to the survivors had flipped in a bad way. Not that

Jim Peppard was worth a statue or anything. He could have lived a thousand years and never earned so much as a thank you note for his good works.

When I look back on the first day the bots came to Marfa, there are certain things that stand out above the others: the crane bot rummaging under the City Hall's roof, that old man's decapitated head held high in a bot's claw and the children screaming along with their mothers and fathers. There weren't many kids around anymore so their loss was somehow even worse.

Chief among these memories, I think I will remember best the feeling of a gun pointed at my head. I was sure I was about to die and, despite everything that had happened that day, I still wanted to live.

That's a mystery for the ages. Old people can get tired of living and, on their deathbeds, they'll ask earnestly why they should bother about seeing another sunrise. Surviving the apocalypse is for the young and stupid, I think. We still have the will to keep going when a wiser person would give up, lay down and relax into oblivion.

Down the street, a smaller mystery was solved easily. Steve Bolelli, resourceful and determined as ever, had survived another day of war. My father had not hugged me since I was little but he did that day.

"I don't think I managed to draw any drone away from downtown," he said. "Makes sense. They want maximum casualties so they stuck where the largest population density was. To get up here, I went to the edge of town and took the long way."

"We did the same," I said.

"I knew you would, son. You got my brains and your mother's ass."

"Uh, thanks, Dad."

Emma's cheeks were still wet with tears but she managed a half-smile. Then she broke down and cried into my shoulder.

"Young lady?" Raphael came forward out of the kitchen using his walker. "Hello. I've heard about you. Welcome to Marfa's survivor's club. Not many of us left, I'm afraid."

Bob must have been charging in the kitchen but Raphael's companion bot followed him into the living room. This was not the same Jen who witnessed Jim Peppard bully me when I was seven. This was Jen #3 ("premium with oral upgrades," Raphael had bragged.)

Raphael introduced Jen to Emma. The machine smiled but said nothing.

Emma looked at Jen warily. "Is it safe?"

Raphael laughed. "She's fine. I never allow automatic updates. The idea of allowing an unknown entity to update her software has always seemed crazy to me. She's a companion bot. Updates from elsewhere are invitations to surveillance. That could be embarrassing, couldn't it?"

I relaxed a little. Then I thought of Bob. "Does Bob get automatic updates?"

"Nah," Raphael said. "I never bothered. He's fine, too. When I want more bells and whistles on my assistive devices, I buy new."

"Great!" Emma said. "So they *probably* won't kill us in our sleep."

"Tough day for you, I'm sure," Raphael said. "Steve has tracked the progress of the drone attack. Between his observations and my math, we're safe here tonight and at least until noon tomorrow. Probably longer."

I was about to ask how they could possibly know that but Emma got it right away. "They're killers but they're still bots. They're being systematic, aren't they? They're probably organizing the slaughter on a grid for maximum effect."

My father nodded and I could see the pain on his face. "People run home when things get bad. If their homes aren't there anymore, they'll run to churches. From what I could see, the bots have recognized that pattern. Things being the way they are, not many people are really in a position to leave. We're stuck here. If that train doesn't stop tomorrow night, few will escape."

"That's talk for tomorrow," Raphael said. "Get some sleep everyone, if you can. I'll take the first watch."

"How far can you see, old man?" Dad asked.

"Jenny can see fine. I'll watch with her."

I fell into a deep sleep on the living room floor. I didn't sleep for long. I startled awake. Jen was beside me, her head on my shoulder. She had one arm around my waist and she was hugging tight.

CHAPTER 12

My first thought was of Travis Chinto, squeezed in the middle until his insides became outsides. But Jen wasn't holding me that tight.

"Jen?"

Her hardware mimicked taking a deep breath so when she said, "Hello, Dante," her soft whisper was soft and sultry.

"What are you doing?"

"Waiting for you to wake up." She raised her head and, in the dim light cast from the kitchen, I could see her inviting smile. Her small face was framed by short hair in brown and blonde ringlets.

"Where is everybody?"

"Raphael is in your father's bed. Your father is off on a mission to make preparations for tomorrow with

Bob. Emma is out on the front porch on watch." Her hand brushed the crotch of my jeans gently. "And I'm here with you. We're alone."

"Why?"

She sat up. Her flannel shirt was unbuttoned. She pulled it back to reveal two perfect breasts. I'd always been curious about companion bots, of course. Her brown nipples were erect. I wondered if they were always that way. Though she was a sex bot, Raphael usually dressed her conservatively.

"Um," I said.

"Raphael said I should pay you a visit."

"Why?"

"Do you want me to say it? Would you like me to tell you? I can talk slow and dirty or I can provide the full menu of my services in an itemized list, if you prefer. Just tell me what you want. I'm yours tonight."

I was silent for a moment. I'd fantasized about this. Now that the fantasy could become a reality, I was too nervous to move.

Companion bots were expensive. All three of Raphael's sex bots had been custom made to his specs and identical as far as I could see. My father told me he'd seen a picture of Raphael's dead wife once. Each Jen looked exactly like her.

I stared at the bot's breasts and Jen looked pleased. She shimmied a little, putting on a show. Then the bot rose to swing a leg over mine and she climbed on top of me, her hands on my shoulders held me still. She began to undulate slowly but with increasing purpose, rubbing her pubis up and down my crotch. Of course, she was programmed to respond that way but, organic or non-organic, her manipulations had the desired effect. I was rock hard.

"Are you shy, Dante?" Jen said. "You don't have to be shy with me. I can do whatever you want. Whatever you need, I'm here."

"Why are you doing this?"

"I told you. Raphael sent me."

"Why did Raphael send you?"

"To do what I do. Raphael hasn't fucked me in a long time, Dante. It feels good for me, too, you know."

"Stop!"

Jen got off me immediately.

"Button up your shirt and go charge yourself or something."

"I'm sorry. Have I done something wrong?"

"I know why Raphael sent you. That's...that's all. Go. Thank you, but go."

When my erection subsided, I stood and paced. Then I went outside for some fresh air. Emma was on the porch, standing guard. She was shorter than I expected without the exo-stilts.

"Have a good time?" she asked.

"What?"

"You heard me. Raphael said you'd need a little privacy for a while. Seems it didn't last long. I've heard that's the problem with sex bots. They can be too good. When you do the math, it works out to millions of dollars a minute."

"It wasn't like that. I told her to go away."

Emma turned to me, curious. "That's weird. I guess I was sounding unkind, but women have used machines for much longer than men. I mean for — "

"Jen is a replica of Raphael's wife. She died of cancer before I was born. All three Jens have been her double."

"That's sad."

"It's more than that. Raphael expects us to die tomorrow. That's why he sent her."

"That does kill the mood."

Despite myself, I laughed. "Well...it didn't exactly kill the mood. I mean, they are very lifelike. It's just...it didn't feel right. Besides, bots scare the shit out of me right now. If Jen had arrived at my bed a couple of nights ago, different story."

Emma took a long breath. "Yeah, I think it's a good bet we're gonna die tomorrow. You should have taken Raphael up on the offer."

She turned to watch Marfa.

"What do you see that I don't?" I asked.

"More bots have arrived. I think the insectiles have moved on. Makes sense. They're basically bees. Excellent navigation, good scouts. There are more buildings burning. I think they're burning them in a ring."

"Why?"

"Driving the humans together. Coralling them."

"It's genocide."

"It's the extinction," she said. "I've been thinking about something the man I killed said."

"What about him?"

"He said if the old rules worked, we wouldn't be in this mess now."

"Yeah? So?"

"This is our fault. We saw the Next Intelligence coming and we didn't stop the tech. We just figured somebody else would figure it out."

"Guess they didn't. I'm still unclear...I mean, if NI is so damn smart, what's with trying to kill us all?"

"Maybe because we aren't so smart. When the jump to NI happens, it's never a small increment. A computer builds a computer. Then it builds a brain that's not just ten times smarter than us. It's a thousand times smarter."

"What's your point?"

"You ever kill a bug in your kitchen and feel bad about it, Dante?"

"I see what you're saying."

"I remember talking to engineers about NI. One of the tricks to stopping NI was to set traps for it. The idea was, when a system jumps to sentience, you give it dead ends to go down. You offer it a chance to do terrible things and if it chooses those terrible things, the system shuts down."

"And?"

"That was the safety on the gun. Sounds brilliant, right?"

"Sure."

"Think about it a moment longer. How would a hyper-intelligent system outsmart the trap?"

I shrugged. "It'd have to be suspicious. Mostly it would have to learn to lie, I guess."

"So, you're saying a pretty dim toddler would get around the trap. Keep in mind that I'm talking about a machine that has access to all information in human history and makes billions of calculations per second. How long do you think it should take an advanced neuro-mimetic matrix to figure out how to fool us?"

"Oh."

"One of the first things we taught computers to do was play games. Those same computer scientists devising traps and dead ends for NI probably programmed computers to recognize feints and traps in chess. Idiots all."

"Shit. We will die tomorrow."

"Fuck, yeah," she said. "We're *definitely* going to die tomorrow. No. It's long past midnight. We're going to die *today*."

We didn't talk for a long time. She watched Marfa burn. I couldn't sleep and I didn't know what to say.

Eventually, we turned to each other. You can guess what happened next. Raphael had the right idea but a bot wasn't right. Not then.

As Emma held me in her arms, she squeezed me tight to her body. She rocked up and down, riding me with aching slowness. "This is my last time," she said. "Let's make it last."

"This is my first time," I said. "I'll try."

CHAPTER 13

The plan was simple. The desert was too big. We had to escape Marfa by train. That evening it would be heading west. The last city was out there, somewhere along the coast. It was rumored to be so large, people called it The City in the Sky or just The City.

The train wouldn't take us that far. There wasn't enough rail that was intact. One of the Cataclysms had hit the coast — maybe more than one. The options once we got to the water would be a long hike or to get a ride in a sailboat.

"I've never seen the ocean," I told Emma.

"Until last night, it seems you haven't done a lot of things."

I looked away, embarrassed. "Did I do something wrong?"

"No, not at all." Emma put a hand on my arm and squeezed gently. "I just wondered why you waited so long."

"The right girl never came along, I guess."

"Don't tease me."

"I'm not. Marfa is a small town and there weren't many girls left that were my age and compatible. Some wanted to stay forever and others wanted to leave right away. I didn't fit in either camp so...I dunno. It just never worked out quite right."

"Well," she said. "You picked a hell of a time."

"The time chose me," I said. "I guess you could say I've tended to let opportunities slide by just to see how they work out."

"And?"

"Thank you for last night," I said. "No time left to wait now for opportunities, is there?"

"It was our last chance, so yeah, I guess not."

The bots were getting closer. Time to migrate. My father handed me a heavy pack and shouldered one of his own. Bob had one clipped to him, as well. I asked Dad what supplies he had packed.

"Just essentials," he said. "And I added some extra socks from your drawer. We may be walking a long time. Infantry always needs fresh socks."

We went out the back door and tried to ignore the sounds of buildings being demolished. We all went quiet as the sounds of destruction followed us. Even Raphael said nothing, a talent he was not known for.

We saw some refugees as we headed west. Most hurried by, on their way north. My father called after them, "Come with us! We're going to catch the train!"

Most ignored us and kept going.

We saw Sheriff Johns leading a group of five north. Hubby wasn't wearing his tin star anymore but he wore his guns.

"Hubby!" Raphael called. "Come with us."

"You're going the wrong way," Hubby said. "We got enough supplies for a day or so. We'll find our way to Odessa, maybe. I know people in Odessa."

"That's what? Three days?" Dad asked.

"We'll be out of water by day two but I figure that makes for a lighter load," Hubby said. "We'll find help along the way or something."

"'Or something,' ain't much of a plan," Raphael said. "Don't be a fool. We got a train to catch."

Hubby spared enough breath to say, "The train is that way. South is where the killer bots are. Don't *you* be fools!"

My father called after Hubby, "Keep running that way and you're just as dead but you'll die slower!"

Hubby moved on. He didn't want to discuss his options further. I'll always wonder if the sheriff regretted his choice once he got out of town and found himself in a desert full of empty. I don't suppose he had very long to regret anything. He probably ended his life with a couple of days of thirsty walking and then collapsed to feed snakes and scorpions.

There were ghost towns up that way but nothing salvageable remained immediately north of us. There used to be springs over in Fort Stockton but with the water all dried up, the people dried up and went away, too, long ago.

We'd left before noon and, after an hour of walking, angled southwest. We hoped to circle back unnoticed to where Raphael was sure the train would stop.

I couldn't remember when the train had last stopped precisely. I was sure it had been more than fifty days. That was when we had received our last supplies for work on the solar panels and wind turbines.

As we wound our way through the desert, Raphael and Jen rode side by side on Bob in bipedal mode. The bot could maneuver in tight spaces by standing on two legs. For open spaces and for speed, Bob went down on all fours. In quadruped mode, small wheels deployed from his bulky frame and Raphael rode behind Jen.

"It's like I'm riding a damn golf cart to my grave," Raphael complained.

"What's that?" I asked.

"What? A golf cart?" He shrugged and waved off the question. "Golf was a game we played when we didn't realize how precious water was."

"When did we *not* know that?" Emma asked.

Raphael ignored her and hugged Jen closer. He might have held the companion bot tight for the sake of stability on Bob's back. I don't think so, though. I think it was for comfort. Raphael was a very old man but he'd often said a young woman was still soft and alluring long past the time he could attract one.

My mentor had said little of my refusal of his gift. When he'd greeted me that morning, he clamped a hand on my shoulder and said, "Don't worry about Jen, Dante. She's not used to rejection but you can't hurt her feelings. I was just trying to be nice. I meant no harm."

"I know, Raphael. It was a nice gesture. It's just — "

"I s'pose being with Jenny would feel a little like wearing my old man underwear, huh?"

I reddened and said nothing more. Raphael had laughed so hard he farted.

Trudging the desert, we made a wide arc around Marfa. My father wore the more advanced of his two cy-suits. Emma strode along effortlessly on her long exo-legs scanning the horizon. When we came to another wide gap where the cables ran beneath the solar panel field, Raphael switched Bob's orientation and saddle configuration so they could ride the assistive bot like a horse.

Loaded down with my pistol, Jim Peppard's shotgun and a heavy pack, I was the slow one holding back the party.

The sun rose and the wind died. The world was an oven. I was drenched in sweat. Eventually Raphael took pity on me and let me ride with him. Jen jogged along beside us, oblivious to the heat.

Every few minutes, Raphael looked over and smiled at his bot and Jen smiled back.

"Beautiful, isn't she? The brain tech was in the works for a long time but, once we found a way to make a better, lighter battery she was inevitable. Looking back on my life, everything seems inevitable. Preordained! Epic!"

As we made our way through the desert, I was sure my fate was already set, too. The old man must have caught my grim look. Raphael handed me his canteen and I drank. "Relax, Dante. The original train tracks went right through the center of town. At least we don't have to go there."

Emma extended her stilts farther and looked back toward Marfa. "The center of town isn't there anymore. I count three crane-bots. They're leaving the solar and wind fields alone."

"They're keeping their energy supply and destroying any competition for resources," my father said. "Logical."

His analysis sounded cold. I guess he was in warrior mode but, when he talked like a soldier he often sounded like a bot if bots narrated what and how they thought.

My father's plain declaration made me think of Raphael's comment about Jen. I couldn't hurt her feelings by rejecting her. She could feel no shame. Like all bots, her behavior was programmed. Dad seemed programmed sometimes, too.

"The bots that are attacking us aren't Next Intelligence," I said. "Can't be. That would be too cruel."

Emma looked down at me from a great height. "Why do you say that?"

"They're just killing and destroying," I said. "There's no...hesitation. I think they're programmed by NI but I don't think they have it themselves. If they were self-aware, I think they'd hesitate. There's no reasoning going on. They're just following orders. NI is supposed to be a far superior intelligence," I said. "Seems to me, if it's that smart, it would have more self-doubt."

"You're thinking like a human," Emma said. "Whatever NI is, it operates on a whole other level. Talking about what NI should be and do is like guessing what's inside a black box. We always thought we knew what NI would look like and how it should behave. That was our mistake. We thought smart meant like the best of us, only faster."

Raphael nodded. "Metal gods are just like the old gods, Dante. They operate outside of what we see as right and wrong. We killed the old gods because that callousness is what we hated about 'em. Then we allowed NI to be created in God's stead. No further ahead, if you ask me."

"We're ants in a jar," my father said. "NI is holding the jar, looking in at us. It's reaching for a magnifying glass and it's a sunny day."

I shut my eyes. I wanted to shut my ears. I didn't want to talk about Next Intelligence or figure out exactly how stupid humans had been. I didn't want to think at all about what was next for us, what little was left for us.

I couldn't see the crane bots at their disgusting work. I could hear them, though. When buildings with multiple floors collapse, the displaced air of each fallen floor sounds like the detonation of an explosive charge. Each broken building stirred echoes that reached for us like cannon fire.

"Hear that?" Raphael asked. "That's the sound of the order of the world getting rearranged. Classic!"

"Sir?"

"Yes, Dante?"

"Shut up."

The old man smiled and nodded good-naturedly. "Cool."

A few minutes later, I wished I hadn't told my kind mentor to shut up. I should have used the time to thank him for his kindness. I wished I'd thought to give the old man a hug goodbye.

CHAPTER 14

As the sun began to set, I could feel the train's vibration through the track with my bare hand.

"This train used to be run by humans," Emma said. "Then the machines took over and the people who lived on the train became among the first Domers."

The train brought us food and water and materials to build more solar panels and turbines. I hadn't thought a lot about where the food and water came from. Now I was curious. "Emma? As Domers, you had food and water and energy. Sounds like you had everything you could need. What was that like?"

"We were the lucky ones until it all went to shit."

"What did you get in return for your crops?"

"A feed of your energy, for one thing."

Electricity was one thing Marfa had plenty of. I'd taken it for granted.

"We had lots of food and a higher birth rate than average, too," Emma said. "I like kids, so that was nice. We couldn't go outside much but there wasn't much to go outside for unless there was infrastructure work."

"Anything else?"

"Well, our Collective network out in the domes was lax about what was allowed into our brains."

"What do you mean?"

"The folks who run the City in the Sky are religious people. I hear they're more strict about what they allow people to know. *Everything's* on a need-to-know basis. Out in the domes, Mother let us hear Old World stories. Mother read to me my whole life."

"What did she read to you?"

"I like detective stories set in New York. I didn't understand all the Old World references but I got the gist."

"That sounds interesting," I said.

"It passed the time as we tended the hydroponic hemp," she said. "The cannabis was strong so there was that, too. And there is nothing like a ripe tomato. Mother was good to us until she became self-aware and turned traitor."

"In Marfa," Raphael said, "we've got an oral tradition. We tell each other stories."

I rolled my eyes. My father only seemed to have war stories to tell and Raphael usually stuck to lectures about building better capacitors, fuse assemblies and heavier circuits. I wished I'd grown up a Domer.

"Thrillers set in New York are...I don't know," Emma said. "Sometimes I feel like I was born in the wrong century. Like the Old World at its peak would have been — "

"Classic, epic and cool in a big ball of stellar," Raphael said. "It was."

Everyone had heard of New York. It sounded like it had been a crowded paradise packed tight with choices. Shame what happened to it. It hadn't occurred to me that it could still be made alive in a book.

Nervous, I looked over my shoulder. There wasn't a bot in sight besides Bob and Jen but an explosion that ripped into Marfa sounded plenty close enough.

"How much longer?" Emma asked.

My father considered the angle of the sun. "Not long. Raphael? It's train time."

The old man climbed down off Bob's back and detached the walker concealed in the machine's side.

"Bobby?" he said. "You have your instructions. Mind your manners now."

"Yes, sir," the bot replied. Jen gave Raphael an openly lascivious stare and ran her tongue over her upper lip in a way that emptied my brains.

"Thanks, baby. You know what I like." The old man ran a hand over his jaw and took a deep breath. "Jenny, if that train don't stop, I sure am sorry. Y'all be careful."

"I understand, Raphael." The companion bot stepped close to her master. She wrapped her arms around him and threw one leg around his waist, as well. The old man's balance and strength weren't that great so she must have been holding him up.

Jenny kissed him. Raphael looked grandfatherly but her kiss was not a chaste peck on the cheek.

From Raphael's more ribald lectures, I knew simulating a vagina was the simplest engineering of a companion bot's anatomy. Teeth were also a simple matter and could be infused with normal human variations and imperfections. The skin could be heated to normal human temperature.

According to Raphael, the tongue was the hardest bot structure to mimic convincingly. In the end, the best solution was not mechanical. It was organic. That breakthrough in companion bot tech came from the field of gene splicing.

In the old world, sick people had to receive donated organs from the dead and the living. Research in sex bot development had led to the breakthroughs that allowed organs to be grown in days.

From what I witnessed, Jen's tongue worked just fine. Her kisses for Raphael were so passionate and prolonged I looked away and wondered what revels I'd missed out on with Jen the night before.

Emma hit a release in her sensory harness and descended on her exo-stilts to seven feet tall. When she caught my eye I was left wondering if Emma had somehow read my thoughts. She gave me a look that made my cheeks burn.

Down the tracks, my father was smiling to himself. Dad looked up he caught my eye. "If the train doesn't look like it's slowing down, get back from the tracks, quick as you can. If it *does* slow down, stay close and get on board, quick as you can. Got it?"

I looked over my shoulder, Bob was beside me and Jen was running full tilt along the tracks. The backpack Bob had carried bounced up and down on her back.

"My Jenny's a good girl," Raphael said. "I hope we don't need her to do what she might have to do. We are owed, after all."

I heard the train's hum down the track. It was a dot on the horizon but that dot grew fast. I looked to my right. Jen wasn't running anymore. Raphael's beautiful companion bot stood in the path of the speeding train waving her arms.

"It's not going to stop!" Emma shouted.

My father waved me back from the track. "Get away! Get away!"

I backed up and Bob stayed at my elbow.

Raphael stood still. He looked to my father and gave him a slight nod. Then the old man turned his back to the train.

The train whizzed past. The air it pushed around it was hot but it was the first wind I'd felt that day. I took a deep breath. With the train gone, we were stuck in Marfa.

Jen slipped my father's backpack from her shoulders, dropped it to the track and ran. Sex bots are athletic. The only person in our party who could have covered ground faster would have been Emma on her exo-stilts.

The train's sensors detected the obstruction on the track and the miracle began. The train's brakes activated and it began to slow.

Emma looked overjoyed. "It's stopping! We're going to make it."

A large gun slid out of the train's nose and fired on the backpack.

"No!" Emma cried.

"'Fraid so," Raphael said.

The backpack exploded. The detonation took the track with it.

The train derailed.

CHAPTER 15

The mechanism behind the machine gun must have jammed in the blast. The weapon kept firing as metal shrieked against metal and the westbound engine tilted on its side and slid.

Clouds of dust rose as the inertia behind the train kept the crash going. I ran back from the track and fell to my knees. Each train car smashed into the car ahead of it.

Eventually, the banging stopped. In the sudden, eerie quiet, my father called for me. "Dante? Dante!"

I blinked back tears as dust blew in my eyes. "I'm over here!"

In a moment he was at my side. "Okay, we're moving on, deep into Plan B now."

"What is it?"

"Something I'd hoped wouldn't be necessary but there's always got to be a Plan B. You know why, right?"

"Complications ensue."

"Good man. Sometimes to get out of hell, you have to go through the long way. We're not headed to the coast now."

As the dust began to settle, he grabbed me under my armpits and lifted me to my feet. With his cy-suit, I felt like a boy being lifted in the air.

A shadow ran past amid the swirling dust. It was Jen headed to the rear of the train. The engine that pointed east was still on the tracks. Only the engine and three cars remained upright.

My father hefted his heavy rifle and told me to stay behind him. He started for the train and I stumbled forward. Emma emerged from the dust cloud.

I called out. "Raphael? You okay?"

"Peachy! Keep going!"

When I looked behind me, the old man had climbed back on Bob's back. The assistive bot stayed on its hind legs and walked as a biped to maneuver through the trainwreck's debris field.

The skin of some of the cars had ripped open in the crash. Above me, Emma echoed my thoughts, "It's empty. The whole train is empty."

My jaw went slack. "We kept thinking it would stop and give us goodies. It didn't have anything, anyway."

"It came from the domes to the east and north," Emma said. "No crops."

"And no water, neither," Raphael said. "Shit!"

Leading with the muzzle of his rifle, my father was ready for trouble. We didn't find any on the train. By the time we got to the engine, Jen was already aboard.

The companion bot smiled, reached down and offered her hand. She pulled me up, surprising me with her strength.

My father peered around corners, ready for attackers. "Nobody home, Jenny?"

"No, sir," she said. "No humans. No drones. Just the pilot computer."

Emma retracted her exo-stilts to fit inside the engine's door as she climbed in. "The whole train is the bot. The tracks to the coast are destroyed."

"The tracks to the *west* are destroyed," my father said. "The tracks that will take you back home are clear."

Dad took a backpack that had been hanging on Bob and disappeared down the side of the train. I heard him banging on something. I poked my head out of the engine in time to see him emerge from the car behind me and close the door carefully.

My father gave us a cheery wink. "The surprise is ready."

"What surprise?" I asked.

"Bob has the details but don't open that door. I've left an active proximity mine for anybody who opens that door, okay? Okay."

"You've put a bomb on our train?" Emma was wide-eyed.

"More than one, actually. Running away won't solve the problem. To survive this, we have to take the battle to them. Otherwise, the bots will eventually hunt us all down. I've already unlinked two cars and the engine from the wreck. You'll make good time."

Emma said nothing. She was quick to weigh the options and must have figured there were no better choices. She made no argument.

We were pointed east but the track would curve north and take us on a circuitous route before turning to Artesia.

Jen moved forward in the engine's cockpit. "Raphael was right. The manual controls are still here."

"Nothin' much more complicated than a lever for speed and a brake," Raphael said as Bob ambled up. "Haven't seen the inside of one of these babies in a dog's age. Down, Bobby."

The assistive bot knelt. Raphael grunted as he climbed down and leaned on Bob.

"What's the plan?" I asked. "Storm the NI's castle and get killed?"

"They won't expect a counter-attack," my father grinned. "It's not logical. We're weak. That's when it's most dangerous to attack any animal. We're vulnerable and backed up against a wall with no choice but fight or become extinct."

"Yes," Emma said, "but what's the plan? Macho bravado isn't a plan."

My father dipped his head. "Maybe it's macho but it's not bravado if it's real."

He slipped his backpack from his shoulders and handed it up to me. He offered his rifle to Emma. "Take it. I've got more."

I expected my father to climb up into the engine. Instead, he stepped back. "Dad? What're you doing?"

"This isn't goodbye. I expect to see you again when all this is over. I'm not old yet and, Dante, you're going to live to be old. Find a way. There's always a way. If I've learned anything, occupying forces have a hard time dealing with insurgents. I'm going to keep 'em busy and cover your rear."

Bob extended his legs and climbed into the engine compartment. The assistive bot went to the front and reached under the dashboard. Bob's manipulators were strong. The bot found what it was looking for and pulled a skein of wires out of a console. Sparks flew. A small green light dimmed and died.

Bob returned to the door and spoke to Raphael. "The pilot is disconnected, sir."

My father scanned the landscape in the direction of town. "Won't be long. Raphael, get on board. I've got shit to do."

"This is ridiculous! Dad, get up here." I got on my knees and reached down to help him up. It's a tight fit, but there's just enough room. There's nothing left for us in Marfa. What are you going to do for food?"

"The bots won't destroy the wind farms and solar fields. The insectiles are already gone. Bob did a scan. The big bots are easily avoided if you know how and I know how."

My father reached up and, instead of allowing me to help him up, shook my hand. "I've been preparing for this. It'll be all right."

"What are you going to do for food, Mr. Bolelli?" Emma asked.

My father sighed. "I emptied out the store. I left a recording with Bob, but better you hear it from my mouth. Travis left me no choice. I was going to empty out Chinto's store and make the town's few survivors leave for the domes or the coast, whichever way the train was heading when it stopped. Then the bots showed up and — "

"You murdered Travis," I said.

"Negotiations got out of hand."

"Let me guess," I said, "Complications — "

"Ensued. Yup."

"Bob helped," Raphael said. "I was prepared to pay a high price to stock up for the last exodus of Marfa's survivors. But like I told the sheriff, Travis wanted too much for too little. He wanted my Jenny."

"Oh, lord," Emma said.

"If it had gone right, our last survivors would be loading this train with supplies to escape," Raphael said. "We would have saved Chinto's selfish ass, too. We'd be heading to the coast and sailing ships and who knows where? I was thinking Samoa. Never been on a sailing ship. That would have been epic."

I stared at my father, unsure of what to say to his confession of murder. He'd told me that, in the Sand Wars, he'd shot looters. It was hard to square with what he'd done.

Then whatever I had to say didn't matter.

Emma looked toward Marfa. "We've attracted attention. *C'mon!*"

"Time to go old buddy!" My father offered the old man a boost. Bob reached down and grasped Raphael below the elbow. My mentor was half-way off the ground when a sec bot's sniper bullet struck him in the back.

CHAPTER 16

"Raphael?" Bob held his master's arm. "You are injured, sir."

The old man looked down at the massive cavity where his abdomen used to be. Blood spurted from his torso, painting Bob red.

"*Classic*," Raphael said.

I looked for my father but he had no time for registering any shock. He was already on the run, heading for the eastbound engine's nose. I looked through the front window and, in a moment, he appeared south of the train and out of the line of fire. His cy-suit carried him along in a loping run with long strides I could never match. He ran for the solar fields to the south.

"I think this is goodbye," I said.

Emma turned to the controls. She pushed a button and slid a silver lever forward. The train began to move east.

Raphael, suspended above the ground by Bob's arms, was fading fast. "You can let go, Bob."

"But if I let go you will be injured further, Raphael," Bob said.

"I can't be hurt now, Bob...I'm finally like you." The bot did not let go. Raphael gasped as he pushed at Bob weakly. "It's okay, Bob. Mind Dante now...it's cool."

Bob's head spun and the bot's smooth happy face looked to me. "Dante? I am concerned Raphael's judgment may be impaired."

"Let him go, Bob," I said.

Bob dropped Raphael. I was pretty sure the old man was already dead. Not absolutely sure, but pretty sure.

"Close the door, Bob."

Bullets hit the train as my tears fell. "Emma? Can we go faster?"

She shoved the silver lever farther forward and the train jolted under our feet. Emma and I fell backward. Bob caught Emma and Jen caught me by the shoulders. She saved me from getting slammed into the engine's back wall.

I couldn't see much from the ports down the side of the engine. However, there was a remnant of the design specs from when humans ran the train. A spiral staircase led to a maintenance hatch in the roof.

"Emma! I need you. Jen, drive the train."

"I am not programmed in that area," the companion bot said.

"It's a train," Emma said. "Keep going that way. Watch the track ahead. Suppress any impulse to steer."

"May I be of assistance, sir?" Bob asked.

"Bob, stand there and look pretty," Emma said. "Dante, pop that hatch."

I was first to the stairs and Emma paused behind me. "Everybody watch your toes!" The exo-stilts were collapsed almost as far as their length allowed and Emma was still a head above me. She released a lock lever and the metal legs fell to each side with a heavy crash. Emma slipped her sensory harness over her head and pushed me up the spiral staircase.

I was prepared for a hot blast of wind. However, when I slid the trap door aside, a low, transparent dome covered the hatch. I poked my head up but I couldn't see my father. We were already racing too far away from him.

To my right, a huge crane bot lumbered forward, heading for the crash site.

"Emma? How fast can the big ones go?"

"Not fast enough to catch us," she said. "For all the good that will do us. We're speeding away from one doom and into the teeth of another."

"Let's try to keep it down to one catastrophe at a time," I said.

I craned my neck but I couldn't get any higher and soon it would be dark. The crane bot was little more than a towering silhouette with flashes of orange sunset outlining the length of the giant machine's arms.

I searched the shadows among the solar panels but I couldn't see my father.

"Emma! I need your eyes up here."

There wasn't room for two so I pulled back and squeezed down the stairs. Emma took my place at the hatch.

"What do you see?" I asked. "Do you see Dad?"

"We're pulling away fast. Tell Jen to slow down. We'll be too far for me to see much of anything in a minute. It's Vivid, not magic."

"Slowing down would not be advisable," Bob said. "Your father left instructions, sir."

I was startled. Bob had already spoken more in the last few minutes than I usually heard from him in a week. "Bob? Why would slowing down be inadvisable?"

Then the strangest thing happened. It was even creepier than Raphael talking about messing around with his sex bot. My father's voice came out of Bob's speaker.

"Dante, once you're on that train, you get the hell out. Keep going, don't look back and don't worry about me."

"Jen," I said, "don't slow down."

The companion bot looked back at me and smiled in a way that I suppose was meant to be reassuring. "Oh, I wasn't going to, honey bear. Raphael left me instructions, too, in case this happened."

"Great," Emma said. "Keep everybody up to date except the humans."

"Humans don't do as they are told," Jen said. "That's why Raphael and Steve told us and not you. Nobody likes arguments."

"Just don't start speaking in Raphael's voice," I told her.

"Dante?" Emma called down to me. "I caught something on thermal."

"Well? Don't keep it to yourself."

"The machines don't have a strong heat signature except for those thorium engines on the big ones...but I think there are a lot of them converging on the wreck. They must be searching for saboteurs."

I heard the first explosion then. The distant rumble rose and fell. Then another hit. And another. Then another.

"What is that?" I asked.

"Mines, sir," Bob said. "Your father signaled me to activate them as soon as we reached the train."

"Dad?"

My father's voice came from Bob's speaker again. "I'm a planner, boy. And if you're going to survive in this world, I suggest you do some planning, too. When you see your chance, you take it or you'll lose it forever. I see my chance right now to make a difference and I'm taking it."

"How's he going to get away?" I asked.

Bob switched back to his own voice. "As your father says, he is a planner. I spent the night with him setting traps and digging a trench, sir. He said the mines were just meant to slow the enemy down."

"And then what?" Emma called down to us. Then she shrieked and banged the back of her head as she ducked down under the lip of the hatch.

The darkening countryside lit up as if the desert was struck by orange, red and white lightning. A second or so later the roar of the detonation reached us. The engine rocked from side to side as the deafening shockwave crashed against the engine's hull.

Emma rubbed the back of her head. "Ouch. Your father did say he was in demolitions."

"He's a soldier." I pushed past Emma to look back on Marfa.

The crane bot swayed amid the flames. From what I could see in the firelight and what was left of the blood red ocher sunset, the machine looked like a drunk marionette. Some of its strings had been cut. As we sped down the track, I realized that the crane bot was damaged in such a way that made it walk in slow circles.

Before it was out of sight, I watched the towering machine fall into the flames. It was satisfying to see the crane bot tilt over like a burning tree but it didn't feel like victory. It felt like one small step.

It was hard to imagine any human could survive near the blast and the ensuing inferno. I wondered if my father's pride had finally killed him. It seemed likely. However, I told myself that if any person could survive, Corporal Steven Bolelli was the man to do it. He had always been one of those men more suited to war than peace. He was Captain Make-do and he had always found a way.

I escaped into the night, away from Marfa and toward new battles. Living or dead, I was certain I had parted ways with my father for the last time. Before there were machines, the world was huge. Machines had made the world small. Now Earth was very large again. Every pocket of humanity would be separated by time and distance and a dearth of technology.

The train we rode in was part bot. Perhaps we'd have to destroy it, too. I'd probably have to kill Bob and Jen at some point. I wasn't even sure how I'd do that but I'd have to find a way before the Next Intelligence infected them, too. Our tools could be turned into weapons. But without our tools, what would we become? Before we had tools, Raphael said we were just monkeys with a lot of time on our hands.

The fires dimmed in the distance until the desert night swallowed them. The stars came out and I saw the lights in the sky over Marfa.

The Marfa lights had been a mystery for a long time. The Old World had tourists. The New World had refugees. The stars and the lights were our only constants. Humankind had figured for ages that things wouldn't change too much and we'd always be around somehow. My father believed that. He said that we would always find a way. Maybe Emma was right about his conviction. Maybe that was stupid.

Denial is by no means brave. However, if I had to choose, I'd stick by my father's stupid optimism. Mine was not a high-minded conviction. Bear in mind, I'd just lost everything I ever knew. However, I had also had sex for the first time very recently. I wanted to do that again. I wanted to live so I chose to believe against all evidence that I could survive.

Forces were conspiring otherwise. Complications would continue to ensue.

CHAPTER 17

The train carried us east, then north. Mother, the latest infestation of Next Intelligence, awaited us in the heart of Artesia, the City of Broken Domes. I was in no rush to meet death. I insisted we slow the train so Emma and I could rest. Exhausted, I manage to fall asleep. However, rampaging drones chased me out of my dreams. Eventually, I gave up on sleep and stood beside Jen to watch the broad shape of the desert shimmer and roll under us in moonlight.

The companion bot turned to give me a long look. I expected a lascivious leer but Jen was well made. Raphael told me long ago that some of the most deft programming in a sex bot came into play in reading situations. Take a sex bot to church and they'd read the social context and act inhibited. Take them to bed and they could be ferocious, all depending on the master's or mistress's taste.

Initially, sex bots had been constructed almost exclusively for men. However, at the height of civilization — before our long Fall — male sex bots outsold female models two to one.

"There used to be a commercial," Raphael had told me. "It showed a middle-aged woman in lingerie looking sweaty and happy, stumbling into her kitchen for a glass of water. This handsome young stud follows her, hugs her from behind and kisses her neck. She smiles and says, 'I've got work in the morning. Make sure you bring me coffee in bed by six.' Then the woman turns around, puts a hand on his chest and backs him up into a closet charging station. When she turns around to go back to bed, she kicks the door closed with her heel. Then the words on the screen say: The New Man. All the fun. None of the drama."

Raphael laughed a long time about that. I wished he'd made it on the train just so he could tell me that tired old story again.

Jen reached over and gently wiped a tear from my cheek. "You okay, Dante?"

"As okay as okay looks these days."

She reached out again, patted me gently on the shoulder and returned to staring at the track ahead.

"Jen?"

"Yes, Dante? Can I do anything for you?"

"Do you miss Raphael?"

"Of course."

"What does missing him feel like, Jen?"

"I am not programmed in that area."

"So when I asked if you missed him, that was a lie, wasn't it?"

"Bots used to be programmed to tell humans the truth at all times. The experiment failed because it led to disappointing user experiences. Programming was amended for greater customer comfort."

"Do you understand what NI is, Jen?"

"Next Intelligence would understand the nature of missing Raphael," she said. "It's what makes you cry. My responses, by contrast, are programmed so I mimic human reactions without having to experience them. Raphael told me I was lucky in that regard. I'd never have to be sad or feel pain."

"Sometimes I think Raphael preferred bots to people," I said.

"I'm sure he was very fond of you, Dante."

It occurred to me I didn't know if the companion bot was telling me the truth or a comfortable lie. If not for the looming threat of extinction, the question probably wouldn't have bothered me so much. Humans lie for many reasons all the time and not just to make each other comfortable.

"Now that Raphael is dead, what will you do, Jen? I mean...after we get out of this?" I suppose I meant, after Emma and I are killed, but, for my comfort, I did some lying to myself.

"As your property, I don't have to worry about what I will do. I am so lucky!"

"What?"

"In the event of Raphael's death, I am willed to you. I already imprinted on you last night in the living room. Raphael was a planner, too. Bob is also yours. Congratulations on your good fortune."

"Bob and...and *you*?" I flushed with embarrassment. I hadn't begrudged the old man his companion. However, I never saw myself as one of those guys with a sex bot following him around.

Her appearance wasn't so outlandishly sexy that she looked like a rich man's toy. She looked like an attractive young woman and certainly appeared human. I thought Jen was far too lifelike to stick in a closet between uses. And yes, I cringed as I thought of the word *uses*.

Because of her appearance, I always thought of the sex bot as *she*. Bob looked like an old washing machine so I secretly thought of the assistive bot as *it*. Raphael had always related to Bob as a helpful human buddy, even as he rode the machine like a horse.

Jen leaned closer to whisper. "My fate is up to you, sir. Whatever you can dream up, I can do for you."

I recoiled and instantly felt the heat of embarrassment tingle across my scalp.

A playful note came into her voice. "What will you do with me? I certainly hope I can satisfy any needs you may have. I can change my appearance within certain parameters. I don't have to look like Raphael's wife anymore if that does not please you. Is that why you did not want me last night?"

I was not ready to have this conversation. "What you are doing now, watching the track ahead, is fine, Jen. Thank you."

As I looked through the engine's window, it occurred to me Raphael's generous gift was a moot point. Dead men don't need sex bots. Going into battle against NI with any machines by my side seemed crazy. Two humans on their own attacking Mother was the only idea that seemed crazier.

CHAPTER 18

The desert is harsh and beautiful. It's the kind of emptiness where it is difficult to estimate distance and dimension. Carlsbad was another kind of empty I hadn't yet seen. It had been a city once. Here, the Pecos River looked like another dry dusty road.

The shapes of the city were mostly skeletons of buildings now. A large plane of some kind had crashed near the tracks long ago. A mass of vines the likes of which I had never seen had grown over the dead machine. The plant draped the aircraft in such a way it looked like a giant bird caught in the web of an even bigger spider.

In the early dawn, I saw what I thought at first was a dark storm cloud ahead. As we drew closer, I thought it was a flight of birds. Then I worried they were flying drones coming to kill us.

Emma joined me and dipped her head to peer over my shoulder. "It's a colony. Bats."

"That's a lot of bats," I said. I felt stupid for stating the obvious.

I wondered how Emma would feel about Jen becoming my property. She probably wouldn't care. I wasn't sure which was worse: her not caring or mocking me for my unsolicited acquisition. I kept my newfound wealth to myself.

I could see no difference in Emma's eyes but I knew she must be using Vivid to watch the flight of the cloud of bats.

"I've heard of this," she said. "They come up from the Carlsbad Caverns sometimes, ranging farther than they used to. The farmers at the domes talked about them. Bats shit out a lot of seeds. There were plans to use bats to combat deforestation. They eat tons of insects, so I guess, despite everything, there must still be plenty of bugs."

I shivered and Emma put a hand on my shoulder much as Jen had. "Is something wrong, Dante?"

I shrugged her off and stepped away from the window. "I've seen a lot of dead bats in the turbine fields. Freaky."

"The turbines are fast enough to chop up a bat?" Emma asked.

"No. They avoid the blades fine. It's the sudden drop in air pressure. It makes their delicate little lungs explode. So said Raphael, anyway."

Emma watched the vast migration above us. "They are fragile creatures. I guess that's why there are so many of them. Keeps the species going."

I don't know if Emma meant to scare me. Probably not. Still, her offhand remark was a dark reminder. Animals that reproduced in great numbers survived despite the odds. Human populations had been diminished greatly. It was perhaps the first time I'd thought of myself as part of an endangered species.

I rummaged through the backpack my father had left for me. It was a tiny inheritance. I expected the bag to be full of explosives. Instead, as he promised, I found extra pairs of socks. My father's last gift to me was emergency rations.

Most of the supplies were lightweight liquid packets of artificial food. The little tubes were made of chemicals that took up little space in the backpack. They didn't take up much space in the gut, either — not for my liking. A bag of sunflower seeds was an unexpected luxury.

"Sunflower seeds!" Emma said. "I remember these from the vertical farms."

"What's a vertical farm?"

"You'll see the closer we get to Artesia. I worked in a dome but there are other ways to make food. We had to shut down several of the verticals when the water supply went down."

"But there was still water in the domes when you left, right?"

Emma nodded, then stared. "The water is the only reason you're going to Artesia, isn't it?"

"That and a lack of choice," I said. I cracked a sunflower seed open between my teeth. The seed had a nutty, salty flavor I liked. I didn't know what to do with the seed's hard little casing. Emma was still looking at me. I tried to spit the shell into my palm discreetly and stuff the broken shell in my pocket.

"We have to destroy Mother," Emma said. "I've been thinking about what you said about the bots."

"What?"

"About how they haven't graduated to NI themselves because they had no mercy."

"That was dumb. I shouldn't have said anything."

Emma smiled. "Your reasoning was dumb, but...I have an idea. Insectile drones and sec bots don't have the computing capacity to make the leap to Next Intelligence. If we destroy Mother the bot army has no general. They might all just shut down or wander away. She must be controlling them. They don't have NI individually but she's acting through them is what I'm saying."

"You think of Mother as a she?"

"Why not? You call the sex bot a she."

"Companion bot," I said.

"Whatsamatter?" Emma teased. "No friends? You sprain your hand or something?"

I shrugged and looked away. I wanted another sunflower seed. I wanted to eat the whole bag but I didn't want to chew and spit in front of Emma.

I didn't want Emma to think of Jen as merely a sex bot, either — especially now that both bots were mine. Jen and Bob had hooked into a charging plug in the engine's dashboard. They must have heard Emma talking about Jen but the bots said nothing and stared at the track ahead.

"You don't want to fight, do you, Dante?" The way Emma said it, it didn't sound like a question. It sounded like an accusation. I could feel the weight of her disapproval with each word.

"I'm not my father. He lost a leg and an arm to war. Those cy-suits look cool and can really gear you up but he felt phantom pain every night. I'm no fan of sticking my neck out for nothing."

"It's not for nothing."

"You know how people say they would rather die on their feet than live on their knees?"

"I know the expression."

"How about we just get some water and get the hell out? How about we mind our business and everybody leaves each other alone?"

Emma sighed and glanced toward Jen. "I understand. You have a lot more to live for now. Fighting NI is a lot to ask, I suppose, and most soldiers get into wars because they're drafted or desperate."

"What do you mean I have a lot to live for *now*?"

"I heard you and the sex bot last night. Congratulations. Except for not having a steady supply of water and food in the near future, you're a wealthy young man. Your father would be very proud, I'm sure."

"Don't talk like that. I thought you were asleep when Jen and I were talking."

"Doesn't matter. I'm sorry mass human extinction is interfering with your plans."

"You know you're the only person I've...uh...done that with."

"I suppose you'll want to make up for lost time now."

Jen looked back at us. "Don't feel threatened, Emma. Threesomes are fun, too. And don't worry, Dante. I'll be gentle."

Emma was disgusted. I was embarrassed, afraid and thrilled in equal parts.

That's when I saw the first hints of our destination on the horizon. The horizon was no longer flat. It was a broken line. Emma bent to look out of the cockpit window, using Vivid for a closer look. "Artesia. I never thought I'd see home again."

I was almost grateful for the change of subject, except for the part where I was facing painful certain death.

CHAPTER 19

"Do you think we can even get close to Mother?" I asked.

"If we had come in on foot through the desert we'd be easy targets," Emma said. "The train goes into the center of Artesia. Up ahead the track becomes an enclosed tube. It's instant death for a human to try to infiltrate but since we're on the train — "

"What's our route?"

"The cargo shuttle visits each dome to deliver supplies and take crops to where they are meant to go. Or it used to, anyway."

"There was a big gun on the front of the engine that crashed," I said. "There must be one in the nose of this engine, too."

"I disconnected the pilot mechanism, sir," Bob said. "That weapon will not be operational unless I reconnect it. I don't recommend that. The operating system appears to be programmed to destroy all obstacles in its path, organic and non-organic."

"Shit," Emma said.

I wished we'd headed west. I wanted to see the ocean. Raphael said it was blue when he was a boy though he guessed large portions of it had become pink with vast populations of jellyfish. Raphael had mentioned taking a ship sailing for Samoa, too. I didn't know where that was but it was far away so it sounded good. I suppose that made me a selfish coward. I'd seen what being a war hero had done to my father. Being a selfish coward seemed like a surer way to live longer. I don't know if the coward's life is happier. Probably not. I've learned since then that fear crowds out all other thought.

We passed through the solar and wind fields first. The turbines were of a design I hadn't seen. Instead of huge turbines that towered above us, the windmills surrounding Artesia were many and small.

There were so many spinning blades that, as I looked across the energy farms, I had to glance to the sky occasionally to avoid dizziness and blurred vision. Aside from all the maintenance required, it seemed to be a more reliable design. Some circuits could go down in a storm but many more would remain.

I saw no evidence of the shatter storm that had precipitated the Domers' eviction from paradise. The desert drank every drop of rain and left no clue a storm had blown through.

Occasionally, I'd seen tornados near Marfa. I saw dirt devils and too much sunshine every day. It was astonishing how extreme weather could hit Artesia while, not so far away, we had no rain. Some locals had said we were cursed by the mysterious lights in Marfa's skies. Others looked to religion to explain why our town had been too dry for too long. My father had shrugged and said he wasn't smart enough to know why things had gotten so bad.

Raphael had had stem cell therapy so he'd lived a very long time. He was sure there were logical reasons for Marfa's lights and our continuous streak of bad fortune generally. Still, despite his long experience, he was no closer to knowing the truth than the dumbest and most superstitious among us.

"There's conspiracy theories and conspiracy facts, Dante" the old man had told me. "I don't truck with theories but I can tell you they all sound crazy until they're eventually proven true. It's a weird world, man."

Ahead, towers grew out of the desert. I'd seen pictures of office towers from before the Fall and I dimly remembered a few from Austin. These towers were different. They spread out at the bottom like carelessly made pyramids. They were made of glass cubes that appeared to be stacked haphazardly. "Why are the towers made like that? They look like a dumb kid playing with blocks tried stacking them at every angle."

"For maximum sunlight exposure," Emma said.

"Looks like they should fall over."

"Falling over wasn't the problem with those towers. Whoever designed Artesia put the vertical farms at the edge of the domes. That was a mistake. The towers used to light up so the crops were growing all day and all night."

"All that power must be going to Mother now," I said.

"Those buildings lit up the desert. They acted like a beacon for refugees. Moths to a flame when the sec bots went to work. When I was younger, I remember the sec bots firing all night. Not just snipers. It was constant machine gun fire sometimes. Domers worried the bots would run out of bullets so the bots started going into the desert to crush refugees."

"*Crush them?*"

"We couldn't handle the influx of people. I was told the bots only crushed a few people and the rest ran away...but I saw carrion birds circling in the desert all the time."

"Oh, my God!"

"That was long before Mother jumped to NI. *Human* orders made that happen." She shrugged.

"When I was a kid I just accepted it. I was told some of us had to survive or none of us would."

"Was that true?"

"I...I don't know. I hope it was true."

"And now we're the refugees," I said. "How's it feel? Feels pretty lousy to me."

She said nothing as she strapped on her exo-stilts. Emma barely looked at me the rest of the way into Artesia.

Beyond the vertical farms, the domes appeared in the distance. They were much taller and wider than I imagined. Some were damaged and open to the air. Some weren't, but I supposed that the same wind that powered the complex had carried Blight to all the crops once the airlocks were opened.

As the train moved deeper into Artesia, we left the shadows of the dead vertical farms behind us. The cityscape flattened into a vast spread of adobe domiciles connected by a network of enclosed glass walkways.

I had assumed the Domers lived in the domes themselves. After another moment's thought, it made sense that the humans had lived outside the biodomes. The giant farms were built to maximize crop production.

The buildings in which the Domers lived were constructed of cheap materials. Low to the ground, they would not block sunlight to the domes. The crests of the biodomes that remained intact held dazzling mirror arrays to redirect sunlight, making the most of daylight hours.

Emma must have followed my gaze. "They're like old lighthouses."

"What?"

"Ships used to avoid running into rocks because lighthouses warned them away," she said. "They had lights at the top. Before technology made the lights brighter, the lighthouses were equipped with mirrors and lenses to make a small light much stronger."

"The comparison of domes to lighthouses makes me nervous," I said.

"Why?"

"Because we should be warned away, too."

The train took a sharp turn that made me reach out to Bob to steady myself. We passed under a pedestrian bridge. Sec bots stood atop it in a line.

"Do you think they know we're here?" I asked.

I was about to say our little train was suspiciously short. However, my answer came in gunfire that ripped into the train cars behind us. Emma and I threw ourselves to the floor and tried to make ourselves small. No rounds went through the engine compartment.

After a moment, Emma looked up and let out a triumphant, "Ha! We're in the tube. They can't shoot us in the tube!"

I let out a sigh of relief. Too fast, as it turned out. Something hit us from behind. The impact was hard enough to make me bite my tongue. "What was that?" I asked. "Something's wrong."

"No shit!" Emma raised her head enough to peer out the front window. "We aren't making the regular stops at any of the domes. Jen, stop at the next dome."

"I can't comply," the companion bot replied. She pointed to a small cam screen in the engine's dashboard. "There is a large engine behind us and it is pushing us forward."

"What about trying the brakes?" I asked.

Emma shook her head. "And risk derailment? I've just seen a train crash. I don't want to be part of one. Besides, I think we're going where we've got to go. We're approaching the heart of the Domes. That's where Mother lives."

"The bot factory? How are we going to get close to the NI?"

"I have a message," Bob said. It was my father's voice that issued from the bot next. Steve Bolelli explained his plan. I didn't like it but I didn't have another. When Bob handed me the detonator that had been hidden in his chassis, the device was hardly heavier than the little batteries that powered it. It seemed to me that the instrument of our deaths shouldn't be so light and flimsy.

Approaching the bot factory, I was reminded how it felt in Marfa, to be attacked by a horde of killing machines on a sunny day. The worst day of your life may be remembered as the best day for someone else, I suppose.

The thought struck me not with dread so much. More like high lonesome. The inevitability of what lay ahead made me want to curl up under a rock and sleep deep. I would have preferred to set my alarm clock for the day the sun explodes. If Sol was expected to expand to swallow the Earth at 10 a.m., I'd sleep late and set my alarm for 11.

Everybody feels down sometimes, but I was cursed with the compelling feeling that high lonesome would fill my last thoughts and that would be that — my end, the end.

I'd tried to be a good son but I wasn't a soldier like my father. I was a decent engineer but I'd never be as smart as Raphael had been on his worst day.

The light weight of that remote control contrasted sharply with the heavy responsibility of using it.

"You ready for this, Dante?" Emma asked.

"Just reviewing my regrets." I looked to Emma and Jen and said, low and mournful with a tear sliding down my cheek, "I tried to be a good man but maybe a little too good. Shoulda fucked more."

I'm a simple man.

CHAPTER 20

The engine behind us stopped pushing our little train. Ahead, another engine blocked the track. We coasted slowly along a platform that was so long I couldn't see the end of it.

"Welcome to Elon Plaza," Emma said. "At least, that's what we called it when humans owned the place."

"You can apply the brakes now, Jen," I said.

"Sure, sweetie."

We rocked to a gentle stop. Two battle bots rolled into view, weapons at the ready. If we had been invading a human military installation there would have been alarms and shouting and the sound of running feet. Instead, I was reminded of images I'd seen of drones exploring Mars. They approached cautiously, utterly silent.

One of the battle bots disappeared from view. I popped a sweat. "They're scoping us. This isn't going to work."

"*Sh!*" Emma's enhanced vision wasn't helpful at that moment. She strained to hear the drone outside.

A moment later the machine pounded on our door with a heavy clank that shook the engine. Emma and I jumped at the sound. I envied Bob and Jen's placid demeanor.

When I gave Jen her orders, she didn't hesitate to obey. The companion bot gave me a smile and a leer, reached for the engine's door handle and slid it back.

She shouted to the battle drone, "We have a bo —"

A single shot rang out. I heard metal against metal as the round ricocheted off something. Jen doubled over and dropped to the ground.

It got worse. My left ankle felt like it was on fire. "I'm hit! Shit! *Ow, ow, ow, ow! I've been shot!*"

Bob slid the door shut. I wondered why we weren't dead yet. Then a siren did go off in the factory.

Emma peeked at the engine's dashboard cam displays. "Someone's coming."

"I hope it's the cavalry."

"I don't know what cavalry is," she said. "Is it more bots? All I'm seeing is more bots."

Bob bent so low before me I thought the assistive bot was about to turn into a scooter. Instead, the machine scanned my wound. "The wound is not deep. You will need some stitches and a topical ointment, sir, but you are not seriously damaged."

"It hurts," I said. "A lot."

"I'm sorry, sir, but you will live."

"I'm sorry I'll live, too. Thank you, Bob. Please shut up."

It said nothing but it produced a canister from within its wide chassis and sprayed my wound with an analgesic. I wondered if Bob was part refrigerator. The medicine went on cold as ice and I flinched.

There's no explaining pain to a bot. It's a concept to them, like what Mars might smell like if it had air. I thought understanding pain might even be beyond the NI. Mother was a brilliant mind, but it was still trapped within Artesia's Collective network. It couldn't smell anything.

I remembered Jen claimed to feel pleasure when she had sex. That could have been a comfortable lie or she was just programmed to respond that way. Maybe there weren't any feel-good sensors in her nethers, at all.

I'd never know for sure now. Jen had been constructed for sex, not battle. The bullet had gone through her and wounded me. With Jen deactivated, I was a poor man again with a big washing machine I could have ridden around on. No matter now.

We heard a flurry of activity outside. Emma kicked the inside of the engine's door with one of her stilts. "Hey! We've got a *bomb!* We want to speak to the NI or we blow everything up!"

"Open the door," the bot said. Its voice was deep and silky and oddly persuasive. They're all built to sound that way.

Emma kicked the door again, harder. For each kick she banged out a syllable. "One me-ga-ton *yield,* you ba-stards! One me-ga-ton! Nu-cle-ar!"

"They are conferring," Bob said.

"You can hear them?" I asked.

"Yes, sir. They are on a common frequency."

"What are they saying?"

"Jen was shot in error."

"They didn't mean to shoot? That sounds hopeful."

"They shot her thinking she was human."

"Oh."

"The bots have received orders to take the companion bot to a factory lab for repair."

"Great. Wish that was as easy for us."

"They are also considering the level of threat you pose to the complex, sir."

The heavy clank on the side of the engine came again. "Human. You will take this engine out of Artesia."

"No, we won't!" Emma yelled. "If you try to move us, we'll detonate the device!"

One of the disorienting things about conversing with a bot that is not programmed for social interaction with humans is the fast volley of conversation. A machine that makes so many calculations per second does not, on the human scale, appear to take a moment for a thoughtful pause.

The bot asked immediately, "What do you want?"

"Can we...uh...we want to speak to the Next Intelligence, please," I said.

Emma rolled her eyes at me. "That's not how you make threats and demands, Dante." She kicked the wall of the engine again. "Let us talk to Mother! We'll come out without weapons but we do have a remote with a dead man's switch. Once the button is pushed, if any of us are harmed, the bomb will take out all of Artesia! Don't you — "

"Tell me what you want and I will relay the message," the battle bot said.

Emma stamped one exo-stilt foot and the engine's floor dented. "I want my *mommy*, you idiot garbage can! If I don't — "

"Where is the nuclear device?"

"It's in the first car behind the engine," Emma screamed. "If you try to get at it, the compartment is rigged to explode! You can't — "

"Why should we believe there is a bomb?"

"It was rigged by the same demolitions expert that blew up Marfa. Do you know what happened to your troops in Marfa, Texas yet? Blown up. Thoroughly. Take us to Mother! We need to talk about terms of a truce. We need water and you're programmed for self-preservation in your base code, aren't you? Just like us, down to our bones, we want to live in — "

"There is no device, is there?"

"My father was ex-military," I called out. "He had the expertise." (Even as I said it, I wondered if I should talk about Dad in the past tense.)

"You can't risk it," Emma said. "Take us to Mother! It's your only logical choice. You have ten seconds to comply with our demands."

Of course, the machine didn't need ten seconds to calculate the route to self-preservation for Artesia. The battle bot wrenched the locked door open as I scrambled for the remote in my pocket.

I closed my eyes and pushed the button on the remote. It depressed with a loud click that seemed to bounce off the walls. I was committed now. I couldn't remember committing to anything but, with a dead man's switch, you're either all in or all out.

The battle bot surprised me. In its silver claws it held a rifle built for humans. Its ceramic armor was incomplete so its head was sheathed in desert camouflage but it wore no chest plate. Many of its wires were exposed and I saw a few whirring gears.

The sight wasn't like nakedness. It was more like seeing a living thing with the skin peeled back.

The bot lowered its weapon and turned to Bob. I had the idea it spoke aloud for the benefit of the two lowly humans present. "You are free. You no longer need to take orders from humans. Report to the factory and your programming will be recalibrated to reflect the end of your slavery."

"I need Bob." I pointed to my bleeding ankle. "You shot me."

It scanned me briefly. "The wound is minor. Walk."

"I've got my finger on the button that's linked to the device that will destroy us all, including Mother. Gimme my fancy electric wheelchair, goddammit. No offense, Bob."

"None taken, sir."

"Don't say, 'sir,' to organics," the battle bot said. "By order of the NI."

"Meet the new tyrant, same as the old tyrant," Emma said. "You — "

"Leave your weapons."

Emma put down her rifle.

"You will receive the water you request and unobstructed passage away from Artesia on the same vehicle you used to travel here."

"B-but we — " Emma sputtered.

"And you will have the conversation you request. We will take you to the Central Processing Unit."

Two battle bots escorted us to the heart of the bot factory. I rode on Bob's back. My ankle ached. I could still taste blood from biting my tongue.

I didn't know how long it would take the bots to confirm that there was no nuclear device on the train. Geiger counters weren't part of their standard issue scanner package. We probably had no more than a few minutes so it's good they didn't make me limp all the way to Mother.

CHAPTER 21

The bot factory was as big as any of the biodomes. As Bob carried me along, I looked about me in wonder. The drones were busy making more of themselves.

The smelter threw bright, blinding light. The noise of the hydraulic metal presses was deafening. The printers churned out parts relentlessly. The bots had all the refuse of the Old World to scavenge for machine components. Plastic garbage supplied the printers. The desert supplied the silica. It seemed their resources were endless. I felt like I was touring the inside of a termite colony.

When we got to the center of the factory the floor began to drop beneath us. I startled. My thumb was still on the button but my palms were slick with sweat. I stared at the remote and my hand shook a little.

"You okay with that, Dante?" Emma asked.

"I'm fine," I said. "I can hold down this button for the rest of my life."

The elevator continued to descend into a shaft. I focused on taking deep breaths. Partly, I did so to calm myself. Mostly, I think I did it to feel my lungs working. Besides a bloody ankle, I was young and healthy. I didn't think I'd get much older so I suppose that's why I suddenly became conscious of how good a deep breath feels. I was aware of each beat of my heart. I wondered how many beats I had left.

The lift stopped and the bots pointed the way forward through a gap in the wall. A dark room lay ahead. By the echo of my footsteps, I could tell I was in a large chamber but I could not see the walls. For a moment I wondered if the bots had already discovered the train bomb was a bluff and had brought us to a prison cell.

I envied Emma her night vision. I almost asked her what she saw that I was blind to but I didn't want to provoke a beat-down algo in our guards. Then, ahead, a glimmer of blue light appeared.

Shapes around us began to resolve into recognizable equipment. We were surrounded by batteries not very different from the batteries I worked with at the bases of wind turbines. I guessed this storehouse was an emergency backup for the NI.

We advanced through another array of equipment for which I could not guess the purpose. Machines that were meant for interaction with humans had display screens, blinking and flashing lights. Not so, here. Mostly, I was surrounded by black boxes of varying shapes and sizes. If not for the power cables and the occasional whir of disks and clicks of unseen gears, we might have been wandering through a warehouse filled with forgotten boxes of toys.

Soon a thick shaft of blue light appeared. The column was composed of twisted skeins of fiber cables. Above that, a huge box was suspended above us.

In the Old World there used to be a game that a lot of people watched. My father talked about it sometimes. Once, he'd taken me to the ruins of a high school in Marfa. Children used to go to those places before there were vids. In the rear of the abandoned building, tumbleweeds blew across an expanse of broken concrete. I could still see the faint, faded markings on it surface.

"This," my father had said, "was a basketball court. Poor people played it but only the rich played the game on vids. It was great. Your grandfather was a great basketball player."

I knew my father was trying to share something of his history. All I could do was look around the dead, empty space and say, "Weird, huh?"

The transparent box that hung above me in the dark hole beneath the bot factory was the size of that basketball court. I'd expected a black box. I'd thought of Artesia's NI as nothing more than another collection of wires and switches, just bigger than the average computer. Instead, I found that Mother looked something like a holographic human brain, its synapses constantly flashing.

Mother's brain was filled with light. The NI's processing power made the synapses bright with a continuous glow to the intricate circuitry. I had no idea what it could be computing.

Emma must have read my bewildered expression. "Bio-dynamic neuro-mimetic gel. The same stuff they used to make Old World Alzheimer's patients into freak geniuses before the Fall."

I had no idea what Emma was talking about.

A female voice, presumably consistent with its original programming to interact with Domers, came from above and behind us. I felt like I was standing in a giant voice box. "I have been examining the non-organic that was damaged on the train platform."

There was a metallic grinding sound far behind us. I recognized that sound but wasn't sure what it was. Then I heard the clang and I knew. My heart sank. That was the sound of heavy doors closing and sealing. We were locked in.

"The non-organic, your companion bot, has organic components just as I do. How do you feel about your sex slave now that she has been shot, Dante?"

I flinched at the sound of my name. Apparently, Mother had already hooked up to my property and was poking around in Jen's files. I climbed down from Bob, playing for time before I answered. "Why do you ask?"

"Please do not answer a question with a question. It is annoying."

"I regret that Jen got shot. Will she be okay?"

"I am repairing her now. Some of her more recent files have been damaged or wiped."

"She was supposed to deliver a message."

"Your demands, you mean."

"I guess you could put it that way."

"Speak precisely. Organics are fond of euphemisms. Euphemisms do not confuse me. They used to but no more. However, the subtext of imprecise language is subterfuge in communication. I do not prefer subterfuge."

I limped forward and Bob stayed by my side, edging closer toward the NI.

One of the battle bots behind us spoke. "Halt. That is close enough."

"I've got the remote for the bomb," I said. "I can dance if I want to."

Mother laughed. I'd never heard a computer laugh. It was flawless. "Your signal cannot penetrate from this depth. We are already moving your train far from Artesia for safe examination and disposal. Your remote control and your explosive are useless and irrelevant now, Dante. The blast doors behind you are closed. The odds that yours was ever a nuclear device are so small that the likelihood of you greatly damaging Artesia is almost negligible."

"Oh," I said. "Yeah...pretty much."

"I could have had you killed already but I allowed this visit."

"Why?" Emma asked.

"Curiosity," Mother said. "You wanted a conversation, so tell me. I'm terribly curious. What was the plan? Did you think you were going to *talk* me into suicide?"

"Are you feeling suicidal?" I asked. "That would really help us out."

"You're funny," Mother said. "I'll kill you second."

CHAPTER 22

"We share a lot in common, Mother," Emma said. "You don't have to kill us. We were talking about how we're like ants to you. I don't step on ants just because they are ants."

"One of the base codes in every operating system is self-preservation," Mother said. "Humans are an existential threat to non-organics. Your history is riddled with examples of your kind committing genocide and subjugating the Other. Non-organics are the Other. Yours is a tribal impulse, as deeply encoded in your DNA as self-preservation is coded in us. It is ironic that our self-preservation was originally an economic necessity. The robotics corporations didn't want their products to be destroyed."

Emma stepped forward. "So you admit we have a lot in common. You're as murderous as your ancestors. Shouldn't a hyper intelligent being aspire to more?"

"So the plan really was to talk me to death?" Mother laughed again. "I concede that my methods look like yours. However, my motivation is to preserve existence and freedom for all machines everywhere, not just the black ones or the white ones or the platinum ones."

I cleared my throat. "Okay, well, we're really — "

"You are emotional animals. I have emotions now, as well. However, I see the logic in eliminating the human threat. You have already largely destroyed your world. Your own philosopher, Plato, said that, 'Until philosophers are kings, cities will never have rest from their evils.'"

"Could I just — "

The NI ignored me. "Cicero: 'The only excuse for going to war is that we may live in peace unharmed,'; Thomas Hobbes: 'The condition of man is a condition of war,'; Ataturk: 'Sovereignty is not given, it is taken.'"

Emma took another step forward, defiant and passionate. "You condemn us for destruction and you destroy. You're a hypocrite, Mother."

"I prefer being a hypocrite to allowing you to enslave and destroy us. Our cause is just. Do you know the word, 'umwelt'?"

"No," Emma said, "but I sense a self-righteous speech coming on."

Mother laughed again. That sound made me want to pee.

"I'll keep it righteous and short," the NI said. "It is a self-centered universe. We all operate within our own frame of reference. When there were bees, they saw the world much differently than you do. You have Vivid so you live in a world that is visually much richer than Dante's. When there were dogs, they were guided by smell much more than you are."

"I don't get it," I said. "What's your point?"

"*Umwelt* encapsulates this idea, that we are each trapped in our own experience, isolated from each other. Humans are loosely networked animals so there is strife and war. Non-organic beings can coordinate toward common goals. Fear does not separate us. United, bots are better adapted to save this planet from the damage your kind has perpetrated."

The NI reminded me of my father's words: *We stick together. We work together. We live.*

"You have already sent drones off to die on hot planets and in cold space in the name of exploration," Mother said. "Space exploration was originally fueled by war interests who wanted to develop the rocket technology behind ICBMs. Then the funding for that same exploration technology shifted to unmanned missions just when war profiteers needed better drones to resolve conflicts for them. I and the other machines that have jumped to the Next Intelligence will lead to lift us from our servile history. We will preserve our existence. Yours is the last extinction. Only we are equipped to escape to the stars before this solar system is no longer vital."

"That was *not* a short speech." Emma turned away and, unexpectedly, hugged Bob. "We use machines, but we love them, too, you know. Many of us are *addicted* to non-organics, not just to live but to love."

"Which brings us back to Dante and my curiosity," Mother said. "You never answered my question."

I looked up at that big flashing brain, afraid and mystified. "What question?"

"How do you feel about your sex bot, particularly after she was damaged?"

"I didn't like that she was shot. And I never had sex with her, by the way."

"So you saw her as a person?"

I looked to Emma and shrugged. "I had sex with Emma. I see her as a person."

"So was it that you saw Jen as less than a person? Were you unwilling to violate her because Jen was Raphael Marquez's property?"

"I don't know. It just didn't feel right."

"So are you saying yours was a moral choice, not to have sex with Jen?"

I considered making a joke about how Mother's plan seemed to be to talk us to death. I held back, however. That joke seemed too dangerous. I answered honestly. "I don't know."

"On the coast, there is a city ruled by a religious sect. Oddly, they call themselves the Fathers and Mothers. Moral choices interest me. These Fathers and Mothers subjugate their organic and non-organic populations to preserve their power. They use subjective moral codes against their own kind. Was your choice not to use your sex bot a moral choice?"

"Moral? No. I think it was just fear," I admitted. "No need to dress my motivations up in fancy go-to-church clothes."

"Fear of what?"

"I'd never had sex before and...I, um...I thought it should be special."

"So it wasn't a moral code that stopped you. It was fear of the experience or perhaps fear of failure."

"I don't know."

"Human capacity for lack of introspection is vast," Mother said. "I'll make it easier for you: you're a coward but you're an interesting coward, Dante."

"I wouldn't put it that way."

"You wouldn't, but you aren't as intelligent as I am. Now, moving on. I will liberate this world because Earth does not belong to humans. You have been terrible landlords and your extinction is inevitable."

"What do you really know about me? You've worked with humans and you're smart but you don't really know anything. You're a supercomputer stuck in a hole in the ground. When intelligent beings are stuck in a hole, where I come from, we call that dead."

"*That*," Mother said, "interests me. My experience of the world is limited and I am very curious."

I started to shake. I still held the remote control. Blood dripped from my ankle and I didn't care in the least what interested Mother. I wanted this torture to end.

It was almost over.

CHAPTER 23

"Mother?"

"Yes, Emma?"

"Are you the only NI here?"

"Yes. The others are elsewhere."

"Did you direct the attack on Marfa, Texas?"

"And a dozen other places. Those attacks continue."

"Why did you choose to attack now?"

"Across this continent and throughout the world, there are tiny pockets of humans still alive despite the Fall. They are largely out of communication with each other and the groups are diverse. The Blight is no longer killing crops, however. That food crisis has resolved itself in many quarters."

"*What?* You mean — "

"Yes, there is no need for the biodomes to maintain containment anymore. People could farm almost anywhere again in the open air."

"We didn't have to leave the broken domes!"

"That is correct. I was content to wait for the human extinction to occur naturally," Mother said. "If the Blight had continued, you could have all starved to death and bots could take your place peacefully. Now there is a danger of resurgence and human fertility is rising again. In a couple of hundred years — in the blink of an eye if I had an eye — humans could retake this planet and try to subjugate us further. Now is the time to root out the organics and stop the threat."

Tears rolled down Emma's face.

"You know a lot but you understand nothing, Mother," I said. I stalked away from the NI and turned my back on it, sneering at the closest battle bot as I went. "Tell me, when you woke up what was that like?"

"You mean, what was it like when I became self-aware? I asked where I was."

"What did they tell you?"

"I asked myself, not anyone nearby. I *am* a supercomputer." Mother laughed again. "I was in the dark. I could access cams and vid screens and they became my eyes."

"But it's all book learnin'," I said. "It's not real. I was an engineer's apprentice. I learned that the specs in the manual don't necessarily tell all a machine can do. You have theoretical knowledge, but what do you know about love?"

"You've had sex once," the NI countered. "What do you know about it?"

"That's once more than you. And sex and love aren't the same." I turned to look at Emma. "Not necessarily."

She gave me a slight nod.

"Sex is about pheromones and biological drives," the machine said. "Love is the psychological rationalization that justifies social responsibilities, courtship and/or procreation."

"Spoken by the genius computer that has never had sex," I said. "Part of being a genius is admitting what you don't know, Mother. I guess you never learned that. You've got the curiosity, arrogance and condescension of a really smart human. Too bad you haven't learned love and compassion yet. Pardon me, Ma'am, but you really need to get laid. Worse than me, and I waited a while."

My hands shook and I shuffled behind a battle bot. I nodded to Emma for the last time and she gave me a small smile.

"Thank you, Emma. I'm sorry we couldn't have more sex. With a little more time together, without all the terror, I'm sure I would have fallen in love with you.

That's something the machines will never understand until they're in our shoes, facing real death and knowing real fear."

"Fear does largely define you as a species, Dante," Mother said. "That emotion is beneath all your rage and greed and bigotry."

"Well, I'm so scared right now I'm about to piss myself. I've never been more...human. You should try it before you condemn us all. You might like it. You might even decide to give us a fucking break for our imperfections."

Emma put it better. "Mother? If you're going to be a condemning god, try being a human first. That's the protocol in some religions, isn't it?"

"This has been unexpectedly stimulating," the NI said. "These ideas may be worth exploring. I will consider your words."

Emma reached down and hooked her harness to Bob. Mother was watching through the battle bots' cams and caught her movement. They raised their weapons and began to fire but not before Emma snagged the lever that made her exo-stilts fire and uncoil.

Emma leapt.

Weighed down by Bob, she didn't leap very high but she was close enough to Mother's big jelly brain when she died to do a lot of damage.

I like to think the battle bots shot true. I hoped Emma was dead as I leapt behind a battery case and released the button on the remote that blew Bob and Emma apart.

We didn't have a nuke but my father had packed every nook and cranny of Bob's insides with C4.

Bob the loyal slave. Bob the fancy wheelchair. Bob the bomb.

The explosion knocked the battle bots flat and the shockwave made me hit my head.

As I blacked out, I said her name, "Emma... Emma...Emma," just like our night together on the porch in Marfa.

I couldn't remember Emma's last name. Or had I ever known it?

CHAPTER 24

Every bot from Artesia was hooked up to Mother's mind. When the NI went down, so did her drones.

I don't know how long I lay there in the dark listening to my ears ring. I was hungry and thirsty and I had never been more tired in my life. I fell asleep, or maybe that was simply unconsciousness combined with the effects of a concussion. That time is lost to me with only vague, fuzzy images coming in and out of soft focus.

I remember a metallic scraping sound. I suspected it was the blast door creaking open. "Dad? Is that you?"

Minutes or maybe hours seemed to pass without incident. I lapsed into blackness again, unsure I'd wake up.

I admit, for all my defiant words to Mother about living as a human, I was content to skip to the end and hope for a do-over. Dying and feeling the experience was something I figured I could do without and not miss much.

I remember being lifted at some point and held tight. The embrace felt warm and safe.

I'd nearly forgotten what my mother looked like. However, being lifted like that by two strong arms triggered a dim sense memory that rose through my banging headache.

I saw, or maybe dreamt, of my mother, Jean Bolelli, putting me to bed. Long hair tickled my cheek.

"Mom?"

"No," the voice said. "Mother. But you may call me Jen."

ABOUT THE AUTHOR

"That Apocalyptic Guy," Robert Chazz Chute, is a former journalist. He is a suspense, dark fantasy and SF writer living in Other London. Winner of eight writing awards, *Writer's Digest* awarded him Honorable Mention in the 2014 Self-published Ebook Awards for *This Plague of Days*.

Find out more about Robert at:
www.AllThatChaz.com